John Buchan was born in 187! Childhood holidays were spen had a great love. His passion ɪᴏɪ ᴛʜᴇ reflected in his writing. He was educated at Glasgow University and Brasenose College, Oxford, where he was President of the Union.

Called to the Bar in 1901, he became Lord Milner's assistant private secretary in South Africa. In 1907 he was a publisher with Nelson's. In World War I he was a *Times* correspondent at the Front, an officer in the Intelligence Corps and adviser to the War Cabinet. He was elected Conservative MP in one of the Scottish Universities' seats in 1927 and was created Baron Tweedsmuir in 1935. From 1935 until his death in 1940 he was Governor General of Canada.

Buchan is most famous for his adventure stories. High in romance, these are peopled by a large cast of characters, of which Richard Hannay is his best known. Hannay appears in *The Thirty-nine Steps*. Alfred Hitchcock adapted it for the screen. A TV series featured actor Robert Powell as Richard Hannay.

FICTION

THE BLANKET OF THE DARK
CASTLE GAY
THE COURTS OF THE MORNING
THE DANCING FLOOR
THE FREE FISHERS
THE GAP IN THE CURTAIN
GREENMANTLE
THE HALF-HEARTED
THE HOUSE OF THE FOUR WINDS
HUNTINGTOWER
THE ISLAND OF SHEEP
JOHN BURNET OF BARNS
THE LONG TRAVERSE
A LOST LADY OF OLD YEARS
MIDWINTER
THE PATH OF THE KING
THE POWER-HOUSE
PRESTER JOHN
A PRINCE OF THE CAPTIVITY
THE RUNAGATES CLUB
SALUTE TO ADVENTURERS
THE SCHOLAR GIPSIES
SICK HEART RIVER
THE THIRTY-NINE STEPS
THE THREE HOSTAGES
THE WATCHER BY THE THRESHOLD
WITCH WOOD

NON-FICTION

AUGUSTUS
THE CLEARING HOUSE
GORDON AT KHARTOUM
JULIUS CAESAR
THE KING'S GRACE
THE MASSACRE OF GLENCOE
MONTROSE
OLIVER CROMWELL
SIR WALTER RALEIGH
SIR WALTER SCOTT

JOHN BUCHAN

GREY WEATHER

MOORLAND TALES OF MY OWN PEOPLE

HOUSE OF
STRATUS

This edition published in 2008 by House of Stratus, an imprint of Stratus Books Ltd., 21 Beeching Park, Kelly Bray, Cornwall, PL17 8QS, UK.

www.houseofstratus.com

Typeset, printed and bound by House of Stratus.

A catalogue record for this book is available from the British Library and the Library of Congress.

ISBN 07551-170-2-6

TO

MY SISTER

In Memory of Old Moorland Days

CONTENTS

BALLAD FOR GREY WEATHER

Cold blows the drift on the hill,
Sere is the heather,
High goes the wind and shrill,
Mirk is the weather.
Stout be the front I show,
Come what the gods send!
Plaided and girt I go
Forth to the world's end.

My brain is the stithy of years,
My heart the red gold
Which the gods with sharp anguish and tears
Have wrought from of old.
In the shining first dawn o' the world
I was old as the sky –
The morning dew on the field
Is no younger than I.

I am the magician of life,
The hero of runes;
The sorrows of eld and old strife
Ring clear in my tunes.
The sea lends her minstrel voice,
The storm-cloud its grey;
And ladies have wept at my notes,
Fair ladies and gay.

My home is the rim of the mist,
　　The ring of the spray,
The hart has his corrie, the hawk has her nest,
　　But I – the Lost Way.
Come twilight or morning, come winter or spring,
　　Come leisure, come war,
I tarry not, I, but my burden I sing
　　Beyond and afar.

I sing of lost hopes and old kings,
　　And the maids of the past.
Ye shiver adread at my strings,
　　But ye hear them at last.
I sing of vain quests and the grave –
　　Fools tremble, afraid.
I sing of hot life, and the brave
　　Go forth, undismayed.

I sleep by the well-head of joy
　　And the fountain of pain.
Man lives, loves, and fights, and then is not –
　　I only remain.
Ye mock me and hold me to scorn –
　　I seek not your grace.
Ye gird me with terror – forlorn,
　　I laugh in your face.

April 1, 1898.

PRESTER JOHN

Or he, who in the wilderness, where no man travels and few may live, dwelled in all good reason and kindness.
Chronicle of S Jean de Remy.

The exact tale of my misadventure on that September day I can scarcely now remember. One thing I have clear in my mind – the weather. For it was in that curious time of year when autumn's caprices reach their height either in the loveliest of skies or a resolute storm. Now it was the latter, and for two days the clear tints of the season had been drowned in monotonous grey. The mighty hill-streams came down like fields in breadth, and when the wind ceased for a time, the roar of many waters was heard in the land. Ragged leaves blocked the path, heather and bracken were sodden as the meadow turf, and the mountain backs were now shrouded to their bases in mist, and now looming ominous and near in a pause of the shifting wrack.

In the third day of the weather I was tempted by the Evil One and went a-fishing. The attempt was futile, and I knew it, for the streams were boiling like a caldron, and no man may take fish in such a water. Nevertheless, the blustering air and the infinite distance of shadowy hilltop took hold on me so that I could not choose but face the storm. And, once outside, the north wind slashed and buffeted me till my breath was almost gone; and when I came to the river's edge, I looked down on an acre of churning foam and mountainous wave.

Now, the way of the place is this. The Gled comes down from flat desolate moorlands to the narrower glen, which in turn opens upon the great river of the countryside. On the left it is bounded by gentle slopes of brown heather, which sink after some score of miles into the fields of a plain; but to the right there lies a tract of fierce country, rugged and scarred with torrents; while at the back of all rise the pathless hills which cradle the Callowa and the Aller. It is a land wild on the fairest summer noon, but in the autumn storms it is black as a pit and impregnable as a fortress.

As ill fortune would have it, I raised a good fish in my first pool, ran it, and lost it in a tangle of driftwood. What with the excitement and the stinging air my blood grew high, I laughed in the face of the heavens, and wrestled in the gale's teeth for four miles upstream. It was the purest madness, for my casting-line was blown out of the water at almost every gust, and never another fish looked near me. But the keenness abode with me, and so it happened that about midday I stood at the foot of the glen whence the Cauldshaw Burn pours its troubled waters to the Gled.

Something in the quiet strength of the great brown flood attracted me against my better judgment. I persuaded myself that in this narrower vale there must be some measure of shelter, and that in its silent pools there were chances of fish. So, with a fine sense of the adventurous, I turned to the right and struck up by the green meadowlands and the lipping water. Before me was a bank of mist; but even as I looked it opened, and a line of monstrous blue shoulders, ribbed and serrated with a thousand gullies, frowned on my path. The sight put new energy into my limbs. These were the hills which loomed far to the distant lowlands, which few ever climbed, and at whose back lay a land almost unknown to man. I named them to myself with the names which had always been like music to my ear – Craigcreich, the Yirnie, the two Muneraws, and the awful precipice of the

Dreichil. With zest I fell to my fishing, and came in a little to the place where the vale ceased and the gorge began.

Here for the first time my efforts prospered, and I had one, two, and three out of the inky pots, which the spate had ringed and dappled with foam. Then, from some unknown cause, the wind fell, and there succeeded the silence which comes from a soaked and dripping world. I fished on and on, but the stillness oppressed me, and the straight craigs, tipped with heather and black with ooze, struck me with something like awe.

Then, ere I knew, I had come to the edge of the gorge, and was out on the peatmoss which gives the Cauldshaw its birth. Once more there came a clearing in the mist, and hill-faces looked out a little nearer, a little more awful. Just beyond that moss lay their foot, and over that barrier of heath and crag lay a new land which I had not yet seen, and scarcely heard of. Suddenly my whole purpose changed. Storm or no storm, I would climb the ridge and look down on the other side. At the top of the Little Muneraw there rose two streams – one, the Callowa, which flowed to the haughlands and meadows of the low country; the other, the Aller, which fought its way to the very centre of the black deserts, and issued some fifty miles distant on another seaboard. I would reach the top, haply see the sight I had often longed for, and then take my weary way down the Callowa home.

So, putting up my rod and strapping tight my creel, I set my face to the knuckle of these mountains which loomed beyond the bog. How I crossed that treacherous land I can scarcely tell, for the rain had left great lagoons which covered shifting sand and clinging mud. Twice I was bogged to my knees, but by dint of many flying leaps from heather to heather, and many lowly scrambles over loose peat, I came to the hard ground whence the slope began. Here I rested, panting, marvelling greatly at my foolhardiness and folly. When honest men were dwelling in comfort at home, I in my fool's heart chose to be playing cantrips among mosses and scaurs and pathless rocks. I was already soaked and half tired, so in no great bodily ease I set myself to the ascent.

In two hours I had toiled to the front shoulder of the Muneraw, and sat looking down on a pit of mist whence three black lochs gleamed faint and shadowy. The place was hushed save for the croak of ravens and the rare scream of a hawk. Curlews and plovers were left far below; the place was too wild for rushes or bracken; and nothing met the eye but stunted heather, grey lichen-clad boulders, and dark craigs streaked with the fall of streams. I loosened a stone and sent it hurling to the loch below, and in a trice the air was thick with echoes of splash and rush and splinter.

Then once more I set my face to the steep and scrambled upward. And now there came to trouble me that very accident which I most feared; for the wind brought the accursed mist down on me like a plaid, and I struggled through utter blindness. The thickness of mirk is bad enough, but the thickness of white, illimitable ether is worse a thousandfold, for it closes the eye and mazes the wits. I kept as straight as might be for what I knew was the head of the hill, and now upon great banks of rotten granite, now upon almost sheer craigs, I made my track. In maybe an hour the steeps ceased, and I lay and panted on a flat bed of shingle, while the clammy mist drenched me to the bone.

Now for the first time I began to repent of my journey, and took grace to regret my madcap ploy. For the full perils of the place began to dawn upon me. I was here, in this dismal weather, a score of miles from any village, and nigh half as many from the nearest human habitation. A sprain or a broken limb would mean death, and at any moment I might step over a cliff face into eternity. My one course of safety lay in finding the Callowa springs, and following the trickle to the glens. The way was long, but it was safe, and sooner or later I must come to a dwelling house.

I knew well that the Callowa rose on the south side of the Muneraw, and the Aller somewhere on the north. But I had lost all sense of direction, I had no compass, and had it not been for the wind, I should have been without guidance. But I remembered that it had blown clear from the north on all my way up the Gled, and now, as I felt its sting on my cheek, I turned with it to what I guessed to be the south. With some satisfaction I began to descend, now sliding for yards, now falling suddenly in a rocky pool, whence a trickle issued among a chaos of stones. Once I came to a high fall, which must have been wonderful indeed had the water been of any size, but was now no more than a silver thread on a great grey face. Sometimes I found myself in ravines where the huge sides seemed to mock the tiny brawling water. A lurking fear began to grow upon me. Hitherto I had found no loch, though I had gone for miles. Now, though I had never been at Callowa head, I had seen it afar off, and knew that the Back Loch o' the Muneraw lay near the source. But now the glen was opening, peat and heather were taking the place of stone, and yet I had seen no gleam of water.

I sat down to consider, and even as I looked the mist drew back again. And this was what I saw. Brown bog lay flat down a valley, with a stream in its midst making leaden pools. Now there are bogs and bogs, and some are harmless enough; but there was that in the look of this which I could not like. Some two miles down the stream turned, and a ridge of dark and craggy hills fronted the eye. Their edges were jagged, and their inky face was seamed and crossed with a thousand little cataracts. And beneath their shadow lay the cruel moss, with flows and lochs scattered over it like a map on a child's slate.

To my wonder, in the very lee of the hill I saw what seemed to be a cottage. There was a stunted tree, a piece of stone wall, and a plain glimpse of a grey gable end. Then I knew whither I had come. The wind had changed. I had followed north for south, and struck the Aller instead of the Callowa. I could not return over that fierce hill and those interminable moorland miles. There was naught to be done save to make for the stones, which might be a dwelling. If the place was ruined, I would even sleep the night in its shelter, and strive to return in the morning.

If it was still dwelled in, there was hope of supper and bed. I had always heard of the Aller as the wildest of all waters, flowing, for most of its course, in a mossland untenanted of man. Something of curiosity took me, in spite of my weariness, to meet with a dweller in this desert. And always as I looked at the black hills I shuddered, for I had heard men tell of the Caldron, where no sheep ever strayed, and in whose sheer-falling waters no fish could live.

I have rarely felt a more awful eeriness than in crossing that monstrous bog. I struck far from the stream, for the Aller, which had begun as a torrent, had sunk into links of unfathomable moss-holes. The darkening was coming on, the grim hills stood out more stark and cruel, and the smell of water clung to my nostrils like the odour of salt to a half-drowned man. Forthwith I fell into the most violent ill temper with myself and my surroundings. At last there was like to be an end of my aimless wanderings, and unless I got through the moss by nightfall, I should never see the morning. The thought nerved me to frantic endeavour. I was dog-tired and soaked to the marrow, but I plunged and struggled from tussock to tussock and through long black reaches of peat. Anything green or white I shunned, for I had lived too long in wildernesses to be ignorant that in the ugly black and brown lay my safety.

By and bye the dusk came, and a light was kindled in the cottage, at which sign of habitation I greatly rejoiced. It gave me new heart, and when I came to a more level place I ran as well as my wearied legs would suffer me. Then for my discomfiture I fell into a great bed of peat, and came out exceeding dirty. Still the flare grew nearer, and at last, about seven o'clock, just at the thickening of darkness, I reached a stone wall and a house end.

At the sound of my feet the door was thrown open, and a string of collies rushed out to devour me. At their tail came the master of the place, a man bent and thin, with a beard ragged and torn with all weathers, and a great scarred face roughly brown with the hill air and the reek of peat.

"Can I stay" – I began, but my words were drowned in his loud tone of welcome.

"How in the warld did ye get here, man? Come in, come in; ye'll be fair perished."

He caught me by the arm and dragged me into the single room which formed his dwelling. Half a dozen hens, escaping from the hutch which was their abode, sat modestly in corners, and from a neighbouring shed came the lowing of a cow. The place was so filled with blue fine smoke that my eyes were dazed, and it was not till I sat in a chair by a glowing fire of peats that I could discern the outlines of the roof. The rafters were black and finely polished as old oak, and the floor was flagged with the grey stones of the moor. A stretch of sacking did duty for a rug, and there the tangle of dogs stretched itself to sleep. The furnishing was of the rudest, for it was brought on horseback over barren hills, and such a portage needs the stoutest of timber. But who can tell of the infinite complexity of the odour which filled the air, the pungency of peat, varied with a whiff of the snell night without and the comfortable fragrance of food?

Meat he set before me, scones and oaten-cakes, and tea brewed as strong as spirits. He had not seen loaf-bread, he told me, since the spring, when a shepherd from the Back o' the Caldron came over about some sheep, and had a loaf-end for his dinner. Then, when I was something recovered, I sat again in the fireside chair, and over pipes of the strongest black we held high converse.

"Wife!" he said, when I asked him if he dwelt alone; "na, na, nae woman-body for me. I bide mysel', and bake my bakings, and shoo my breeks when they need it. A wife wad be a puir convanience in this pairt o' the warld. I come in at nicht, and I dae as I like, and I gang oot in the mornings, and there's naebody to care for. I can milk the coo mysel', and feed the hens, and there's little else that a man need dae."

I asked him if he came often to the lowlands.

"Is 't like," said he, "when there's twenty mile o' thick heather and shairp rock atween you and a level road? I naether gang there, nor do the folk there fash me here. I havena been at the kirk for ten 'ear, no since my faither dee'd; and though the minister o' Gledsmuir, honest man, tries to win here every spring, it's no' often he gets the length. Twice in the 'ear I gang far awa' wi' sheep, when I spain the lambs in the month o' August, and draw the crocks in the back-end. I'm expectin' every day to get word to tak' off the yowes."

"And how do you get word?" I asked.

"Weel, the post comes up the road to the foot o' the Gled. Syne some o' the fairmers up the water tak' up a letter and leave it at the foot o' the Cauldshaw Burn. A fisher, like yersel', maybe, brings it up the glen and draps it at the herd's cottage o' the Front Muneraw, whaur it lies till the herd, Simon Mruddock, tak's it wi' him on his roonds. Noo, twice every week he passes the tap o' the Aller, and I've gotten a cairn there, whaur he hides it in an auld tin box among the stanes. Twice a week I gang up that way mysel', and find onything that's lyin'. Oh, I'm no' ill off for letters; I get them in about a week, if there's no' a snawstorm."

The man leant forward to put a fresh coal to his pipe, and I marked his eyes, begrimed with peat smoke, but keen as a hawk's, and the ragged, ill-patched homespun of his dress. I thought of the good folk in the lowlands and the cities who hugged their fancies of simple Arcadian shepherds, who, in decent cottage, surrounded by a smiling family, read God's Word of a Saturday night. In the rugged man before me I found some hint of the truth.

"And how do you spend your days?" I asked. "Did you never think of trying a more kindly countryside?"

He looked at me long and quizzically.

"Yince," he said, "I served a maister, a bit flesher-body doun at Gled-foot. He was aye biddin' me dae odd jobs about the toun, and I couldna thole it, for I'm a herd, and my wark's wi' sheep. Noo I serve the Yerl o' Callowa, and there's no' a body dare say a word to me; but I manage things according to my ain guid juidgement, wi'oot ony 'by your leave'. And whiles I've the best o' company, for yince or twice the Yerl has bided here a' nicht, when he was forewandered shooting amang thae muirs."

But I was scarce listening, so busy was I in trying to picture an existence which meant incessant wanderings all day among the wilds, and firelit evenings, with no company but dogs. I asked him if he ever read.

"I ha'e a Bible," he said doubtfully, "and I whiles tak' a spell at it to see if I remember my schulin'. But I'm no keen on books o' ony kind."

"Then what in the name of goodness do you do?" said I.

Then his tongue was unloosed, and he told me the burden of his days; how he loved all weather, fighting a storm for the fight's sake, and glorying in the conquest; how he would trap blue hares and shoot wildfowl – for had he not the Earl's leave? – and now and then kill a deer strayed among the snow. He was full of old tales of the place, learned from a thousand odd sources, of queer things that happened in these eternal deserts, and queer sights which he and others than himself had seen at dawning and sunset. Some day I will put them all down in a book, but then I will inscribe it to children and label it fantasy, for no one would believe them if told with the circumstance of truth. But, above all, he gloried in the tale of the changes of sky and earth, and the multitudinous lore of the hills. I heard of storms when the thunder echoed in the Caldron like the bleating of great sheep, and the man sat still at home in terror. He told with solemn eyes of the coming of snow, of masterful floods in the Aller, when the dead sheep came down and butted, as he said, with their foreheads against his house wall. His voice grew high, and his figure, seen in the red glare of the peats, was like some creature of a tale.

But in time the fire sank, the dogs slumbered, our pipes went out, and he showed me my bed. It was in the garret, which you entered by a trap from the shed below. The one window had been shattered by some storm and boarded up with planks, through whose crevices I could see the driving mist and the bog lying dead under cover of night. I slept on rough blankets of homespun, and ere I lay down, in looking round the place, I came upon a book stuck fast between the rafters and the wall. It was the Bible used to brush up the shepherd's learning, and for the sake of his chances hereafter I dragged it forth and blew the dust from it.

In the morning the mist had gone, and a blue sky shone out, over which sudden gusts swept like boats on a loch. The damp earth still reeked of rain; and as I stood at the door and watched the Aller, now one line of billows, strive impetuous through the bog-land, and the hills gleam in the dawning like wet jewels, I no more wondered at the shepherd's choice. He came down from a morning's round, his voice bellowing across the uplands, and hailed me from afar. "The hills are no vera dry," he said, "but they micht be passed; and if I was sure I wadna bide, he wad set me on my way." So in a little I followed his great strides through the moss and up the hill-shoulder, till in two hours I was breathing hard on the Dreichil summit, and looking down on awful craigs, which dropped sheerly to a tarn. Here he stopped, and, looking far over the chaos of ridges, gave me my directions.

"Ye see yon muckle soo-backit hill – yon's the Yirnie Cleuch, and if ye keep alang the taps ye'll come to it in an 'oor's time. Gang doun the far shouther o't, and ye'll see a burn which flows into a loch; gang on to the loch-foot, and ye'll see a great deep hole in the hillside, what they ca' the Nick o' the Hurlstanes; gang through it, and ye'll strike the Criven Burn, which flows into the Callowa; gang doun that water till it joins the Gled, and syne ye're no' abune ten mile from whaur ye're bidin'. So guid-day to ye."

And with these lucid words he left me and took his swinging path across the hill.

AT THE ARTICLE OF DEATH

" Nullum
Sacra caput Proserpina fugit."

A noiseless evening fell chill and dank on the moorlands. The Dreichil was mist to the very rim of its precipitous face, and the long, dun sides of the Little Muneraw faded into grey vapour. Underfoot were plashy moss and dripping heather, and all the air was choked with autumnal heaviness. The herd of the Lanely Bield stumbled wearily homeward in this, the late afternoon, with the roof-tree of his cottage to guide him over the waste.

For weeks, months, he had been ill, fighting the battle of a lonely sickness. Two years agone his wife had died, and as there had been no child, he was left to fend for himself. He had no need for any woman, he declared, for his wants were few and his means of the scantiest, so he had cooked his own meals and done his own household work since the day he had stood by the grave in the Gledsmuir kirkyard. And for a little he did well; and then, inch by inch, trouble crept upon him. He would come home late in the winter nights, soaked to the skin, and sit in the peat-reek till his clothes dried on his body. The countless little ways in which a woman's hand makes a place healthy and habitable were unknown to him, and soon he began to pay the price of his folly. For he was not a strong man, though a careless onlooker might have guessed the opposite from his mighty frame. His folk had all been short-lived, and already his was the age of his father at his death. Such a fact might have warned him to circumspection; but

13

he took little heed till that night in the March before, when, coming up the Little Muneraw and breathing hard, a chill wind on the summit cut him to the bone. He rose the next morn, shaking like a leaf, and then for weeks he lay ill in bed, while a younger shepherd from the next sheep farm did his work on the hill. In the early summer he rose a broken man, without strength or nerve, and always oppressed with an ominous sinking in the chest; but he toiled through his duties, and told no man his sorrow. The summer was parchingly hot, and the hillsides grew brown and dry as ashes. Often as he laboured up the interminable ridges, he found himself sickening at heart with a poignant regret. These were the places where once he had strode so freely with the crisp air cool on his forehead. Now he had no eye for the pastoral loveliness, no ear for the witch-song of the desert. When he reached a summit, it was only to fall panting, and when he came home at nightfall he sank wearily on a seat.

And so through the lingering summer the year waned to an autumn of storm. Now his malady seemed nearing its end. He had seen no man's face for a week, for long miles of moor severed him from a homestead. He could scarce struggle from his bed by midday, and his daily round of the hill was gone through with tottering feet. The time would soon come for drawing the ewes and driving them to the Gledsmuir market. If he could but hold on till the word came, he might yet have speech of a fellow man and bequeath his duties to another. But if he died first, the charge would wander uncared for, while he himself would lie in that lonely cot till such time as the lowland farmer sent the messenger. With anxious care he tended his flickering spark of life – he had long ceased to hope – and with something like heroism looked blankly towards his end.

But on this afternoon all things had changed. At the edge of the water-meadow he had found blood dripping from his lips, and half-swooned under an agonising pain at his heart. With burning eyes he turned his face to home, and fought his way inch by inch through the desert. He counted the steps crazily, and with pitiful sobs looked upon mist and moorland. A faint bleat of a sheep came to his ear; he heard it clearly, and the hearing wrung his soul. Not for him any more the hills of sheep and a shepherd's free and wholesome life. He was creeping, stricken, to his homestead to die, like a wounded fox crawling to its earth. And the loneliness of it all, the pity, choked him more than the fell grip of his sickness.

Inside the house a great banked fire of peats was smouldering. Unwashed dishes stood on the table, and the bed in the corner was unmade, for such things were of little moment in the extremity of his days. As he dragged his leaden foot over the threshold, the autumn dusk thickened through the white fog, and shadows awaited him, lurking in every corner. He dropped carelessly on the bed's edge, and lay back in deadly weakness. No sound broke the stillness, for the clock had long ago stopped for lack of winding. Only the shaggy collie which had lain down by the fire looked to the bed and whined mournfully.

In a little he raised his eyes and saw that the place was filled with darkness, save where the red eye of the fire glowed hot and silent. His strength was too far gone to light the lamp, but he could make a crackling fire. Some power other than himself made him heap bog-sticks on the peat and poke it feebly, for he shuddered at the ominous long shades which peopled floor and ceiling. If he had but a leaping blaze he might yet die in a less gross mockery of comfort.

Long he lay in the firelight, sunk in the lethargy of illimitable feebleness. Then the strong spirit of the man began to flicker within him and rise to sight ere it sank in death. He had always been a godly liver, one who had no youth of folly to look back upon, but a well-spent life of toil lit by the lamp of a half-understood devotion. He it was who at his wife's deathbed had administered words of comfort and hope; and had passed all his days with the thought of his own end fixed like a bull's eye in the target of his meditations. In his lonely hill-watches, in the weariful lambing days, and on droving journeys to faraway towns, he had whiled the hours with self-communing, and self-examination, by the help of a rigid Word. Nay, there had been far more than the mere punctilios of obedience to the letter; there had been the living fire of love, the heroical altitude of self-denial, to be the halo of his solitary life. And now God had sent him the last fiery trial, and he was left alone to put off the garments of mortality.

He dragged himself to a cupboard where all the appurtenances of the religious life lay to his hands. There were Spurgeon's sermons in torn covers, and a dozen musty "Christian Treasuries". Some antiquated theology, which he had got from his father, lay lowest, and on the top was the gaudy Bible, which he had once received from a grateful Sabbath class while he yet sojourned in the lowlands. It was lined and relined, and there he had often found consolation. Now in the last faltering of mind he had braced himself to the thought that he must die as became his possession, with the Word of God in his hand, and his thoughts fixed on that better country, which is an heavenly.

The thin leaves mocked his hands, and he could not turn to any well-remembered text. In vain he struggled to reach the gospels; the obstinate leaves blew ever back to a dismal psalm or a prophet's lamentation. A word caught his eye and he read vaguely: "The shepherds slumber, O King…the people is scattered upon the mountains…and no man gathereth them…there is no healing of the hurt, for the wound is grievous." Something in the poignant sorrow of the phrase caught his attention for one second, and then he was back in a fantasy of pain and impotence. He could not fix his mind, and even as he strove he remembered the warning he had so often given to others against deathbed repentance. Then, he had often said, a man has no time to make his peace with his Maker, when he is wrestling with death. Now the adage came back to him; and gleams of comfort shot for one moment through his soul. He at any rate had long since chosen for God, and the good Lord would see and pity His servant's weakness.

A sheep bleated near the window, and then another. The flocks were huddling down, and wind and wet must be coming. Then a long dreary wind sighed round the dwelling, and at the same moment a bright tongue of flame shot up from the fire, and queer crooked shadows flickered over the ceiling. The sight caught his eyes, and he shuddered in nameless terror. He had never been a coward, but like all religious folk he had imagination and emotion. Now his fancy was perturbed, and he shrank from these uncanny shapes. In the failure of all else he had fallen to the repetition of bare phrases, telling of the fragrance and glory of the city of God. "River of the water of Life," he said to himself…"the glory and honour of the nations…and the street of the city was pure gold … and the saved shall walk in the light of it…and God shall wipe away all tears from their eyes."

Again a sound without, the cry of sheep and the sough of a lone wind. He was sinking fast, but the noise gave him a spasm of strength. The dog rose and sniffed uneasily at the door, a trickle of rain dripped from the roofing, and all the while the silent heart of the fire glowed and hissed at his side. It seemed an uncanny thing that now in the moment of his anguish the sheep should bleat as they had done in the old strong days of herding.

Again the sound, and again the morris dance of shadows among the rafters. The thing was too much for his failing mind. Some words of hope – "streams in the desert, and" – died on his lips, and he crawled from the bed to a cupboard. He had not tasted strong drink for a score of years, for to the true saint in the uplands abstinence is a primary virtue; but he kept brandy in the house for illness or wintry weather. Now it would give him strength, and it was no sin to cherish the spark of life.

He found the spirits and gulped down a mouthful – one, two, till the little flask was drained, and the raw fluid spilled over beard and coat. In his days of health it would have made him drunk, but now all the fibres of his being were relaxed, and it merely stung him to a fantasmal vigour. More, it maddened his

17

brain, already tottering under the assaults of death. Before he had thought feebly and greyly, now his mind surged in an ecstasy.

The pain that lay heavy on his chest, that clutched his throat, that tugged at his heart, was as fierce as ever, but for one short second the utter weariness of spirit was gone. The old fair words of Scripture came back to him, and he murmured promises and hopes till his strength failed him for all but thought, and with closed eyes he fell back to dream.

But only for one moment; the next he was staring blankly in a mysterious terror. Again the voices of the wind, again the shapes on floor and wall and the relentless eye of the fire. He was too helpless to move and too crazy to pray; he could only lie and stare, numb with expectancy. The liquor seemed to have driven all memory from him, and left him with a child's heritage of dreams and stories.

Crazily he pattered to himself a child's charm against evil fairies, which the little folk of the moors still speak at their play –

"Wearie, Ovie, gang awa',
Dinna show your face at a',
Ower the muir and down the burn,
Wearie, Ovie, ne'er return."

The black crook of the chimney was the object of his spells, for the kindly ingle was no less than a malignant twisted devil, with an awful red eye glowering through smoke.

His breath was winnowing through his worn chest like an autumn blast in bare rafters. The horror of the black night without, all filled with the wail of sheep, and the deeper fear of the red light within, stirred his brain, not with the far-reaching fanciful terror of men, but with the crude homely fright of a little child. He would have sought, had his strength suffered him, to cower one moment in the light as a refuge from the other, and

18

the next to hide in the darkest corner to shun the maddening glow. And with it all he was acutely conscious of the last pangs of mortality. He felt the grating of cheekbones on skin, and the sighing, which did duty for breath, rocked him with agony.

Then a great shadow rose out of the gloom and stood shaggy in the firelight. The man's mind was tottering, and once more he was back at his Scripture memories and vague repetitions. Aforetime his fancy had toyed with green fields, now it held to the darker places. "It was the day when Evil Merodach was king in Babylon," came the quaint recollection, and some lingering ray of thought made him link the odd name with the amorphous presence before him. The thing moved and came nearer, touched him, and brooded by his side. He made to shriek, but no sound came, only a dry rasp in the throat and a convulsive twitch of the limbs.

For a second he lay in the agony of a terror worse than the extremes of death. It was only his dog, returned from his watch by the door, and seeking his master. He, poor beast, knew of some sorrow vaguely and afar, and nuzzled into his side with dumb affection.

Then from the chaos of faculties a shred of will survived. For an instant his brain cleared, for to most there comes a lull at the very article of death. He saw the bare moorland room, he felt the dissolution of his members, the palpable ebb of life. His religion had been swept from him like a rotten garment. His mind was vacant of memories, for all were driven forth by purging terror. Only some relic of manliness, the heritage of cleanly and honest days, was with him to the uttermost. With blank thoughts, without hope or vision, with naught save an aimless resolution and a causeless bravery, he passed into the short anguish which is death.

POLITICS AND THE MAY-FLY

The farmer of Clachlands was a Tory, stern and unbending. It was the tradition of his family, from his grandfather, who had been land steward to Lord Manorwater, down to his father, who had once seconded a vote of confidence in the sitting member. Such traditions, he felt, were not to be lightly despised; things might change, empires might wax and wane, but his obligation continued; a sort of perverted *noblesse oblige* was the farmer's watchword in life; and by dint of much energy and bad language, he lived up to it.

As fate would have it, the Clachlands ploughman was a Radical of Radicals. He had imbibed his opinions early in life from a speaker on the green of Gledsmuir, and ever since, by the help of a weekly penny paper and an odd volume of Gladstone's speeches, had continued his education. Such opinions in a conservative countryside carry with them a reputation for either abnormal cleverness or abnormal folly. The fact that he was a keen fisher, a famed singer of songs, and the best judge of horses in the place, caused the verdict of his neighbours to incline to the former, and he passed for something of an oracle among his fellows. The blacksmith, who was the critic of the neighbourhood, summed up his character in a few words. "Him," said he, in a tone of mingled dislike and admiration, "him! He would sweer white was black the morn, and dod! he would prove it tae."

It so happened in the early summer, when the land was green and the trout plashed in the river, that Her Majesty's Government saw fit to appeal to an intelligent country. Among a people whose

21

politics fight hard with their religion for a monopoly of their interests, feeling ran high and brotherly kindness departed. Houses were divided against themselves. Men formerly of no consideration found themselves suddenly important, and discovered that their intellects and conscience, which they had hitherto valued at little, were things of serious interest to their betters. The lurid light of publicity was shed upon the lives of the rival candidates; men formerly accounted worthy and respectable were proved no better than white sepulchres; and each man was filled with a morbid concern for his fellow's character and beliefs.

The farmer of Clachlands called a meeting of his labourers in the great dusty barn, which had been the scene of many similar gatherings. His speech on the occasion was vigorous and to the point. "Ye are a' my men," he said, "an' I'll see that ye vote richt. Ye're uneddicated folk, and ken naething aboot the matter, sae ye just tak' my word for 't, that the Tories are in the richt and vote accordingly. I've been a guid maister to ye, and it's shurely better to pleesure me, than a wheen leein' scoondrels whae tramp the country wi' leather bags and printit trash."

Then arose from the back the ploughman, strong in his convictions. "Listen to me, you men," says he; "just vote as ye think best. The maister's a guid maister, as he says, but he's nocht to dae wi' your votin'. It's what they ca' inteemedation to interfere wi' onybody in this matter. So mind that, an' vote for the workin' man an' his richts."

Then ensued a war of violent words.

"Is this a meetin' in my barn, or a penny-waddin?"

"Ca 't what ye please. I canna let ye mislead the men."

"Whae talks about misleadin'? Is 't misleadin' to lead them richt?"

"The question," said the ploughman, solemnly, "is what you ca' richt."

"William Laverhope, if ye werena a guid plooman, ye wad gang post-haste oot o' here the morn."

"I carena what ye say. I'll stand up for the richts o' thae men."

"Men!" – this with deep scorn. "I could mak' better men than thae wi' a stick oot o' the plantin'."

"Ay, ye say that noo, an' the morn ye'll be ca'in' ilka yin o' them *Mister*, a' for their votes."

The farmer left in dignified disgust, vanquished but still dangerous; the ploughman in triumph mingled with despair. For he knew that his fellow labourers cared not a whit for politics, but would follow to the letter their master's bidding.

The next morning rose clear and fine. There had been a great rain for the past few days, and the burns were coming down broad and surly. The Clachlands Water was chafing by bank and bridge and threatening to enter the hayfield, and every little ditch and sheep-drain was carrying its tribute of peaty water to the greater flood. The farmer of Clachlands, as he looked over the landscape from the doorstep of his dwelling, marked the state of the weather and pondered over it.

He was not in a pleasant frame of mind that morning. He had been crossed by a ploughman, his servant. He liked the man, and so the obvious way of dealing with him – by making things uncomfortable or turning him off – was shut against him. But he burned to get the upper hand of him, and discomfit once for all one who had dared to question his wisdom and good sense. If only he could get him to vote on the other side – but that was out of the question. If only he could keep him from voting – that was possible but unlikely. He might forcibly detain him, in which case he would lay himself open to the penalties of the law, and be nothing the gainer. For the victory which he desired was a moral one, not a triumph of force. He would like to circumvent him by cleverness, to score against him fairly and honourably on his own ground. But the thing was hard, and, as it seemed to him at the moment, impossible.

Suddenly, as he looked over the morning landscape, a thought struck him and made him slap his legs and chuckle hugely. He walked quickly up and down the gravelled walk. "Losh, it's guid. I'll dae 't. I'll dae 't, if the weather juist hauds."

His unseemly mirth was checked by the approach of someone who found the farmer engaged in the minute examination of gooseberry leaves. "I'm concerned aboot thae busses," he was saying; "they've been ill lookit to, an' we'll no hae half a crop." And he went off, still smiling, and spent a restless forenoon in the Gledsmuir market.

In the evening he met the ploughman, as he returned from the turnip-singling, with his hoe on his shoulder. The two men looked at one another with the air of those who know that all is not well between them. Then the farmer spoke with much humility.

"I maybe spoke rayther severe yestreen," he said. "I hope I didna hurt your feelings."

"Na, na! No me!" said the ploughman, airily.

"Because I've been thinking ower the matter, an' I admit that a man has a richt to his ain thochts. A'body should hae principles an' stick to them," said the farmer, with the manner of one making a recondite quotation.

"Ay," he went on, "I respect ye, William, for your consistency. Ye're an example to us a'."

The other shuffled and looked unhappy. He and his master were on the best of terms, but these unnecessary compliments were not usual in their intercourse. He began to suspect, and the farmer, who saw his mistake, hastened to change the subject.

"Graund weather for the fishin'," said he.

"Oh, is it no?" said the other, roused to excited interest by this home topic. "I tell ye by the morn they'll be takin' as they've never ta'en this 'ear. Doon in the big pool in the Clachlands Water, at the turn o' the turnip field, there are twae or three pounders, and aiblins yin o' twae pund. I saw them mysel' when the water was low. It's ower big the noo, but when it gangs doon the morn, and gets the colour o' porter, I 'se warrant I could whup them oot o' there wi' the flee."

24

"D' ye say sae?" said the farmer, sweetly. "Weel, it's a lang time since I tried the fishin', but I yince was keen on 't. Come in bye, William; I've something ye micht like to see."

From a corner he produced a rod, and handed it to the other. It was a very fine rod indeed, one which the owner had gained in a fishing competition many years before, and treasured accordingly. The ploughman examined it long and critically. Then he gave his verdict. "It's the brawest rod I ever saw, wi' a fine hickory butt, an' guid greenhert tap and middle. It wad cast the sma'est flee, and haud the biggest troot."

"Weel," said the farmer, genially smiling, "ye have a half-holiday the morn when ye gang to the poll. There'll be plenty o' time in the evening to try a cast wi' 't. I'll lend it ye for the day."

The man's face brightened. "I wad tak' it verra kindly," he said, "if ye wad. My ain yin is no muckle worth, and, as ye say, I'll hae time for a cast the morn's nicht."

"Dinna mention it. Did I ever let ye see my flee-book? Here it is," and he produced a thick flannel book from a drawer. "There's a maist miscellaneous collection, for a' waters an' a' weathers. I got a heap o' them frae auld Lord Manorwater, when I was a laddie, and used to cairry his basket."

But the ploughman heeded him not, being deep in the examination of its mysteries. Very gingerly he handled the tiny spiders and hackles, surveying them with the eye of a connoisseur.

"If there's anything there ye think at a' like the water, I'll be verra pleased if ye'll try 't."

The other was somewhat put out by this extreme friendliness. At another time he would have refused shamefacedly, but now the love of sport was too strong in him. "Ye're far ower guid," he said; "thae twae paitrick wings are the verra things I want, an' I dinna think I've ony at hame. I'm awfu' gratefu' to ye, an' I'll bring them back the morn's nicht."

25

"Guid-e'en," said the farmer, as he opened the door, "an' I wish ye may hae a guid catch." And he turned in again, smiling sardonically.

The next morning was like the last, save that a little wind had risen, which blew freshly from the west. White cloudlets drifted across the blue, and the air was as clear as spring water. Down in the hollow the roaring torrent had sunk to a full, lipping stream, and the colour had changed from a turbid yellow to a clear, delicate brown. In the town of Gledsmuir, it was a day of wild excitement, and the quiet Clachlands road bustled with horses and men. The labourers in the fields scarce stopped to look at the passers, for in the afternoon they too would have their chance, when they might journey to the town in all importance, and record their opinions of the late Government.

The ploughman of Clachlands spent a troubled forenoon. His nightly dreams had been of landing great fish, and now his waking thoughts were of the same. Politics for the time were forgotten. This was the day which he had looked forward to for so long, when he was to have been busied in deciding doubtful voters, and breathing activity into the ranks of his cause. And lo! the day had come and found his thoughts elsewhere. For all such things are, at the best, of fleeting interest, and do not stir men otherwise than sentimentally; but the old kindly love of field sports, the joy in the smell of the earth and the living air, lie very close to a man's heart. So this apostate, as he cleaned his turnip rows, was filled with the excitement of the sport, and had no thoughts above the memory of past exploits and the anticipation of greater to come.

Midday came, and with it his release. He roughly calculated that he could go to the town, vote, and be back in two hours, and so have the evening clear for his fishing. There had never been such a day for the trout in his memory, so cool and breezy and soft, nor had he ever seen so glorious a water. "If ye dinna get a fou basket the nicht, an' a feed the morn, William Laverhope, your richt hand has forgot its cunning," said he to himself.

He took the rod carefully out, put it together, and made trial casts on the green. He tied the flies on a cast and put it ready for use in his own primitive fly-book, and then bestowed the whole in the breast pocket of his coat. He had arrayed himself in his best, with a white rose in his buttonhole, for it behoved a man to be well dressed on such an occasion as voting. But yet he did not start. Some fascination in the rod made him linger and try it again and again.

Then he resolutely laid it down and made to go. But something caught his eye – the swirl of the stream as it left the great pool at the hayfield, or the glimpse of still, gleaming water. The impulse was too strong to be resisted. There was time enough and to spare. The pool was on his way to the town, he would try one cast ere he started, just to see if the water was good. So, with rod on his shoulder, he set off.

Somewhere in the background a man, who had been watching his movements, turned away, laughing silently, and filling his pipe.

A great trout rose to the fly in the hayfield pool, and ran the line upstream till he broke it. The ploughman swore deeply, and stamped on the ground with irritation. His blood was up, and he prepared for battle. Carefully, skilfully he fished, with every nerve on tension and ever-watchful eyes. Meanwhile, miles off in the town the bustle went on, but the eager fisherman by the river heeded it not.

Late in the evening, just at the darkening, a figure arrayed in Sunday clothes, but all wet and mud-stained, came up the road to the farm. Over his shoulder he carried a rod, and in one hand a long string of noble trout. But the expression on his face was not triumphant; a settled melancholy overspread his countenance, and he groaned as he walked.

Mephistopheles stood by the garden gate, smoking and surveying his fields. A well-satisfied smile hovered about his

27

mouth, and his air was the air of one well at ease with the world.

"Weel, I see ye've had guid sport," said he to the melancholy Faust. "By the bye, I didna notice ye in the toun. And losh! man, what in the warld have ye dune to your guid claes?"

The other made no answer. Slowly he took the rod to pieces and strapped it up; he took the fly-book from his pocket; he selected two fish from the heap; and laid the whole before the farmer.

"There ye are," said he, "and I'm verra much obleeged to ye for your kindness." But his tone was one of desperation and not of gratitude; and his face, as he went onward, was a study in eloquence repressed.

A REPUTATION

It was at a little lonely shooting box in the Forest of Rhynns that I first met Layden, sometime in the process of a wet August. The place belonged to his cousin Urquhart, a strange man well on in years who divided his time between recondite sport and mild antiquities. We were a small party of men held together by the shifty acquaintance of those who meet somewhere and somehow each autumn. By day we shot conscientiously over mossy hills or fished in the many turbid waters; while of an evening there would be much tobacco and sporting-talk interspersed with the sleepy, indifferent joking of wearied men. We all knew the life well from long experience, and for the sake of a certain freshness and excitement were content to put up with monotonous fare and the companionship of bleak moorlands. It was a season of brown faces and rude health, when a man's clothes smelt of peat, and he recked not of letters accumulating in the nearest post town.

To such sombre days Layden came like a phoenix among moorfowl. I had arrived late, and my first sight of him was at dinner, where the usual listless talk was spurred almost to brilliance by his presence. He kept all the table laughing at his comical stories and quaint notes on men and things, shrewd, witty, and well-timed. But this welcome vivacity was not all, for he cunningly assumed the air of a wise man unbending, and his most random saying had the piquant hint of a great capacity. Nor was his talk without a certain body, for when by any chance one of his hearers touched upon some matter of technical knowledge, he was ready at the word for a well-informed discussion. The meal ended, as it rarely did, in a full flow of conversation, and men rose with the feeling of having returned for the moment to some measure of culture.

The others came out one by one to the lawn above the river, while he went off with his host on some private business. George Winterham sat down beside me and blew solemn wreaths of smoke toward the sky. I asked him who was the man, and it is a sign of the impression made that George gave me his name without a request for further specification.

"That's a deuced clever chap," he said with emphasis, stroking a wearied leg.

"Who is he?" I asked.

"Don't know – cousin of Urquhart's. Rising man, they say, and I don't wonder, I bet that fellow is at the top before he dies."

"Is he keen on shooting?" I asked, for it was the usual question.

Not much, George thought. You could never expect a man like that to be good in the same way as fools like himself; they had better things to think about. After all, what were grouse and salmon but vanities, and the killing of them futility? said Mr Winterham, by way of blaspheming his idols.

"I was writing to my sister, Lady Clanroyden, you know," he went on, "and I mentioned that a chap of the name of Layden was coming. And here she writes to me today and can speak about nothing but the man. She says that the Cravens have taken him up, and that he is going to marry the rich Miss Clavering, and that the Prime Minister said to somebody that he would be dashed if this chap wasn't the best they had. Where the deuce did I leave Mabel's letter?" And George went indoors upon the quest.

Shortly after Layden came out, and soon we all sat watching the dusk gather over miles of spongy moor and vague tangled birchwoods. It is hard for one who is clearly the sole representative of light amid barbarism to escape from a certain seeming of pedantry and a walk aloof and apart. I watched the man carefully, for he fascinated me, and if I had admired his nimble wits at dinner, the more now did I admire his tact. By some cunning art he drove out all trace of superiority from his air; he was the ordinary good fellow, dull, weary like the rest, vastly relishing tobacco, and staring with vacant eyes to the evening.

The last day of my visit to the Forest I have some occasion to remember. It was marked by a display of weather, which I, who am something of a connoisseur in the thing, have never seen approached in this land or elsewhere. The morning had been hazy and damp, with mist over the hilltops and the air lifeless. But about midday a wind came out of the south-west which sent the vapour flying, and left the tops bald and distant. We had been shooting over the Cauldshaw Head, and about five in the afternoon landed on a spur of the Little Muneraw above the tarn which they call the Loch o' the Threshes. Thence one sees a great prospect of wild country, with birchwoods like smoke and sudden rifts which are the glens of streams. On this afternoon the air was cool and fine, the sky a level grey, the water like ink beneath dull-gleaming crags. But the bare details were but a hundredth part of the scene; for over all hung an air of silence, deep, calm, impenetrable – the quiet distilled of the endless moors, the grey heavens, the primeval desert. It was the incarnate mystery of Life, for in that utter loneliness lay the tale of ages since the world's birth, the song of being and death as uttered by wild living things since the rocks had form. The sight had the glamour of a witch's chant; it cried aloud for recognition, driving from the heart all other loves and fervours, and touching the savage elemental springs of desire.

We sat in scattered places on the hillside, all gazing our fill of the wild prospect, even the keepers, to whom it was a matter of daily repetition. None spoke, for none had the gift of words; only in each mind was the same dumb and unattainable longing. Then Layden began to talk, and we listened. In another it would have been mere impertinence, for another would have prated and fallen into easy rhetoric; but this man had the art of speech, and his words were few and chosen. In a second he was done, but all had heard and were satisfied; for he had told the old tale of the tent by the running water and the twin candle-stars in heaven, of morning and evening under the sky and the whole lust of the gipsy life. Every man there had seen a thousandfold more of the very thing he spoke of, had gone to the heart of savagery, pioneering in the Himalayas, shooting in the Rockies, or bearing the heat of tropical sport. And yet this slim townsman, who could not shoot straight, to whom Scots hills were a revelation of the immense, and who was in his proper element on a London pavement – this man could read the sentiment so that every hearer's heart went out to answer.

As we went home I saw by his white face that he was overtired, and he questioned me irritably about the forwarding of letters. So there and then I prayed Heaven for the gift of speech, which makes a careless spectator the interpreter of voiceless passion.

II

Three years later I found myself in England, a bronzed barbarian fresh from wild life in north Finland, and glad of a change to the pleasant domesticity of home. It was early spring, and I drifted to my cousin's house of Heston, after the aimless fashion of the wanderer returned. Heston is a pleasant place to stay in at all times, but pleasantest in spring, for it stands on the last ridge of a Devon moor, whence rolls a wide land of wood and meadow to a faint blue line of sea. The hedgerows were already bursting into leaf, and brimming waters slipped through fresh green grasses. All things were fragrant of homeland and the peace of centuries.

At Heston I met my excellent friend Wratislaw, a crabbed, cynical, hard-working, and sore-battered man, whose excursions in high politics had not soothed his temper. His whole life was a perpetual effort to make himself understood, and as he had started with somewhat difficult theories his recognition had been slow. But it was sure; men respected him sincerely if from afar; in his own line he was pre-eminent, and gradually he was drawing to himself the work in a great office of State where difficulty was equally mated with honour.

"Well, you old madman," he cried, "where have you been lost all these months? We heard marvellous stories about you, and there was talk of a search party. So you chose to kill the fatted calf here of all places. I should have gone elsewhere; it will be too much of a show this week."

"Who are coming?" I groaned resignedly.

"Lawerdale for one," he answered. I nodded; Lawerdale was a very great man in whom I had no manner of interest. "Then there are Rogerson, and Lady Afflint and Charlie Erskine."

"Is that the lot?"

"Wait a moment. Oh, by Jove, I forgot; there's Layden coming, the great Layden."

"I once met a Layden; I wonder if it's the same man."

"Probably – cousin of Urquhart's."

"But he wasn't commonly called 'great' then."

"You forget, you barbarian, that you've been in the wilderness for years. Reputations have come and gone in that time. Why, Layden is a name to conjure with among most people – Layden, the brilliant young thinker, orator, and writer, the teacher of the future!" And Wratislaw laughed in his most sardonic fashion.

"Do you know him?" I asked.

"Oh, well enough in a way. He was a year below me at Oxford – used to talk in the Union a lot, and beat me hollow for President. He was a hare-brained creature then, full of ideals and aboriginal conceit; a sort of shaggy Rousseau, who preached a new heaven and a new earth, and was worshipped by a pack of schoolboys. He did well in his way, got his First and some 'Varsity prizes, but the St Chad's people wouldn't have him at any price for their fellowship. He told me it was but another sign of the gulf between the real and the ideal. I thought then that he was a frothy ass, but he has learned manners since, and tact. I suppose there is no doubt about his uncommon cleverness."

"Do you like him?"

Wratislaw laughed. "I don't know. You see, he and I belong to different shops, and we haven't a sentiment in common. He would call me dull; I might be tempted to call him windy. It is all a matter of taste." And he shrugged his broad shoulders and went in to dress.

At dinner I watched the distinguished visitor with interest. That he was very much of a celebrity was obvious at once. He it was to whom the unaccountable pauses in talk were left, and something in his carefully modulated voice, his neatness, his air of entire impregnability, gave him a fascination felt even by so unemotional a man as I. He differed with Lawerdale on a political question, and his attitude of mingled deference and certainty was as engaging to witness as it must have been irritating to encounter. But the event of the meal was his treatment of Lady Afflint, a lady (it is only too well known) who is the hidden reef on which so many a brilliant talker shipwrecks. Her questions give a fatal chance for an easy and unpleasing smartness; she leads her unhappy companion into a morass of "shop" from which there is no escape, and, worst of all, she has the shrewdness to ask those questions which can only be met by a long explanation and which leave their nervous and short-winded victim the centre of a confusing silence. I have no hesitation in calling Layden's treatment of this estimable woman a miracle of art. Her own devices were returned upon her, until we had the extraordinary experience of seeing Lady Afflint reduced to an aggrieved peace.

But the man's appearance surprised me. There was nothing of the flush of enthusiasm, the ready delight in his own powers, which are supposed to mark the popular idol. His glance seemed wandering and vacant, his face drawn and lined with worry, and his whole figure had the look of a man prematurely aging. Rogerson, that eminent lawyer, remarked on the fact in his vigorous style. "Layden has chosen a damned hard profession. I never cared much for the fellow, but I admit he can work. Why, add my work to that of a first-class journalist, and you have an idea of what the man gets through every day of his life. And then think of the amount he does merely for show: the magazine articles, the lecturing, the occasional political speaking. All that has got to be kept up as well as his reputation in society. It would kill me in a week, and, mark my words, he can't live long at that pitch."

I saw him no more that night, but every paper I picked up was full of him. It was "Mr Layden interviewed" here, and "Arnold Layden, an Appreciation" there, together with paragraphs innumerable, and the inscrutable allusions in his own particular journal. The thing disgusted me, and yet the remembrance of that worn-out face held me from condemning him. I am one whose interest lies very little in the minute problems of human conduct, finding enough to attract me in the breathing, living world. But here was something which demanded recognition, and in my own incapable way I drew his character.

I saw little of him during that week at Heston, for he was eternally in the train of some woman or other, when he was not shut up in the library turning out his tale of bricks. With amazing industry he contrived to pass a considerable portion of each day in serious labour, and then turned with weary eyes to the frivolity in which he was currently supposed to delight. We were the barest acquaintances, a brief nod, a chance good morning, being the limits of our intimacy; indeed, it was a common saying that Layden had a vast acquaintance, but scarcely a friend.

But on the Sunday I happened to be sitting with Wratislaw on an abrupt furze-clad knoll which looks over the park to meadow and sea. We had fallen to serious talking, or the random moralising which does duty for such among most of us. Wratislaw in his usual jerky fashion was commenting on the bundle of perplexities which made up his life, when to us there entered a third in the person of Layden himself. He had a languid gait, partly assumed no doubt for purposes of distinction, but partly the result of an almost incessant physical weariness. But today there seemed to be something more in his manner. His whole face was listless and dreary; his eyes seemed blank as a stone wall.

As I said before, I scarcely knew him, but he and Wratislaw were old acquaintances. At any rate he now ignored me wholly, and flinging himself on the ground by my companion's side, leaned forward, burying his face in his hands.

"Oh, Tommy, Tommy, old man, I am a hopeless wreck," he groaned.

"You are overworking, my dear fellow," said Wratislaw; "you should hold back a little."

Layden turned a vacant face toward the speaker. "Do you think that is all?" he said. "Why, work never killed a soul. I could work night and day if I were sure of my standing ground."

Wratislaw looked at him long and solemnly. Then he took out a pipe and lit it. "You'd better smoke," he said. "I get these fits of the blues sometimes myself, and they go off as suddenly as they come. But I thought you were beyond that sort of thing."

"Beyond it!" Layden cried. "If I had had them years ago it might have saved me. When the Devil has designs on a man, be sure that the first thing he does is to make him contented with himself."

I saw Wratislaw's eyebrows go up. This was strange talk to hear from one of Layden's life.

"I would give the world to be in your place. You have chosen solid work, and you have left yourself leisure to live. And I – oh, I am a sort of ineffectual busy person running about on my little errands and missing everything."

Wratislaw winced; he disliked all mention of himself, but he detested praise.

"It's many years since I left Oxford; I don't remember how long, and all this time I have been doing nothing. Who is it talks about being 'idly busy'? And people have praised me and fooled me till I believed I was living my life decently. It isn't as if I had been slack. My God, I have worked like a nigger, and my reward is wind and smoke! Did you ever have the feeling, Tommy, as if you were without bearings and had to drift with your eyes aching for solid land?"

The other shook his head slowly, and looked like a man in profound discomfort.

"No, of course you never did, and why should you? You made up your mind at once what was worth having in the world and went straight for it. That was a man's part. But I thought a little dazzle of fame was the heavenly light. I liked to be talked about; I wanted the reputation of brilliance, so I utilized every scrap of talent I had and turned it all into show. Every little trivial thought was stored up and used on paper or in talk. I toiled terribly, if you like, but it was a foolish toil, for it left nothing for myself. And now I am bankrupt of ideas. My mind grows emptier year by year, and what little is left is spoiled by the same cursed need for ostentation. 'Every man should be lonely at heart'; whoever said that said something terribly true, and the words have been driving me mad for days. All the little that I have must be dragged out to the shop window, and God knows the barrenness of that back parlour I call my soul."

I saw that Wratislaw was looking very solemn, and that his pipe had gone out and had dropped on the ground.

"And what is the result of it all?" Layden went on. "Oh, I cannot complain. It is nobody's fault but my own; but Lord, what a pretty mess it is!" and he laughed miserably. "I cannot bear to be alone and face the naked ribs of my mind. A beautiful sight has no charms for me save to revive jaded conventional memories. I have lost all capacity for the plain, strong, simple things of life, just as I am beginning to realize their transcendent worth. I am growing wretchedly mediocre, and I shall go down month by month till I find my own degraded level. But thank God, I do not go with my eyes shut; I know myself for a fool, and for the fool there is no salvation."

Then Wratislaw rose and stood above him. I had never seen him look so kindly at anyone, and for a moment his rough, cynical face was transfigured into something like tenderness. He put his hand on the other's shoulder. "You are wrong, old man," he said; "you are not a fool. But if you had not come to believe yourself one, I should have had doubts of your wisdom. As it is, you will now go on to try the real thing, and then – we shall see."

III

The real thing – Heaven knows it is what we are all striving after with various degrees of incompetence. I looked forward to the transformation of this jaded man with an interest not purely of curiosity. His undoubted cleverness, and the habitual melancholy of his eyes, gave him a certain romantic aloofness from common life. Moreover, Wratislaw had come to believe in him, and I trusted his judgment.

I saw no more of the man for weeks, hearing only that his health was wretched and that he had gone for a long holiday to the south. His private income had always been considerable, and his work could very well wait, but his admirers were appalled by the sudden cessation of what had been a marvellous output. I was honestly glad to think of his leisure. I pictured him once more the master of himself, gathering his wits for more worthy toil, and getting rid of the foolish restlessness which had unnerved him. Then came a chance meeting at a railway station, where he seemed to my hasty eyes more cheerful and well looking; and then my wanderings began again, and London gossip, reputation, and chatter about letters were left a thousand miles behind.

When I returned I had almost forgotten his name; but the air of one's own land is charged with memories, and the past rises on the mind by degrees till it recovers its former world. I found Wratislaw looking older, grimmer, and more irritable, ready to throw books at me for tantalising him with glimpses of an impossible life. He walked me fiercely through Hyde Park, full of abrupt questions as of old, and ever ready with his shrewd, humourous comment. Then in my turn, I fell to asking him of people and things, of the whole complication of civilised life from which I had been shut off for years. Some stray resemblance in a passing face struck me, and I asked about Layden.

Wratislaw grunted savagely. "In a way I am grateful to the man for showing me that I am a fool."

"Then he has gone back to his old life?" I asked, not without anxiety.

"Listen to me," he said gruffly. "His health broke down, as you know, and he went abroad to recover it. He stopped work, dropped out of publicity, and I thought all was well. But the man cannot live without admiration; he must be hovering in its twopenny light like a moth round a candle. So he came back, and, well – there was a repetition of the parable of the seven devils. Only he has changed his line. Belles-lettres, society small talk, everything of that kind has gone overboard. He is by way of being earnest now; he talks of having found a mission in life, and he preaches a new gospel about getting down to the Truth of Things. His trash has enormous influence; when he speaks the place is crowded, and I suppose he is in hopes of becoming a Force. He has transient fits of penitence, for he is clever enough to feel now and then that he is a fool, but I was wrong to think that he could ever change. Well, well, the band-playing for the ruck, but the end of the battle for the strong! He is a mere creature of phrases, and he has got hold of the particular word which pleases his generation. Do you remember our last talk with him at Heston? Well, read that bill."

He pointed to a large placard across the street. And there in flaming red and black type I read that on a certain day under the auspices of a certain distinguished body Mr Arnold Layden would lecture on The Real Thing.

A JOURNEY OF LITTLE PROFIT

The Devil he sang, the Devil he played
High and fast and free.
And this was ever the song he made
As it was told to me.
"Oh, I am the king of the air and the ground,
And lord of the seasons' roll,
And I will give you a hundred pound,
If you will give me your soul."

The Ballad of Grey Weather.

The cattle market of Inverforth is, as all men know north of the
Tweed, the greatest market of the kind in the land. For days in
the late autumn there is the lowing of oxen and the bleating of
sheep among its high wooden pens, and in the rickety sale rings
the loud clamour of auctioneers and the talk of farmers. In the
open yard where are the drovers and the butchers, a race always
ungodly and law-despising, there is such a babel of cries and curses
as might wake the Seven Sleepers. From twenty different adjacent
eating houses comes the clatter of knives, where the country folk
eat their dinner of beef and potatoes, with beer for sauce, and the
collies grovel on the ground for stray morsels. Hither come a
hundred types of men, from the Highland cateran, with scarce
a word of English, and the shentleman farmer of Inverness and
Ross, to lowland graziers and city tradesmen, not to speak of
blackguards of many nationalities and more professions.

It was there I first met Duncan Stewart of Clachamharstan, in the Moor of Rannoch, and there I heard this story. He was an old man when I knew him, grizzled and wind-beaten; a prosperous man, too, with many herds like Jacob and much pasture. He had come down from the North with kyloes, and as he waited on the Englishmen with whom he had trysted, he sat with me through the long day and beguiled the time with many stories. He had been a drover in his youth, and had travelled on foot the length and breadth of Scotland; and his memory went back hale and vigorous to times which are now all but historical. This tale I heard among many others as we sat on a pen amid the smell of beasts and the jabber of Gaelic: –

"When I was just turned of twenty-five I was a wild young lad as ever was heard of. I had taken to the droving for the love of a wild life, and a wild life I led. My father's heart would be broken long syne with my doings, and well for my mother that she was in her grave since I was six years old. I paid no heed to the ministrations of godly Mr Macdougall of the Isles, who bade me turn from the error of my ways, but went on my own evil course, making siller, for I was a braw lad at the work and a trusted, and knowing the inside of every public from the pier of Cromarty to the streets of York. I was a wild drinker, caring in my cups for neither God nor man, a great hand with the cards, and fond of the lasses past all telling. It makes me shameful to this day to think on my evil life when I was twenty-five.

"Well, it chanced that in the back of the month of September I found myself in the city of Edinburgh with a flock of fifty sheep which I had bought as a venture from a drunken bonnet-laird and was thinking of selling somewhere wast the country. They were braw beasts, Leicester every one of them, well-fed and dirt-cheap at the price I gave. So it was with a light heart that I drove them out of the town by the Merchiston Road along by the face of the Pentlands. Two or three friends came with me, all like myself for folly, but maybe a little bit poorer. Indeed, I cared

42

little for them, and they valued me only for the whisky which I gave them to drink my health in at the parting. They left me on the near side of Colinton, and I went on my way alone.

"Now, if you'll be remembering the road, you will mind that at the place called Kirk Newton, just afore the road begins to twine over the Big Muir and almost at the head af the Water o' Leith, there is a verra fine public. Indeed, it would be no lee to call it the pest public between Embro' and Glesca. The good wife, Lucky Craik by name, was an old friend of mine, for many a good gill of her brandy have I bought; so what would I be doing but just turning aside for refreshment? She met me at the door verra pleased-like to see me, and soon I had my legs aneath her table and a basin of toddy on the board before me. And whom did I find in the same place but my old comrade Toshie Maclean from the backside of Glen-Lyon. Toshie and I were acquaintances so old that it did not behove us to be parting quick. Forbye the day was chill without; and within the fire was grand and the crack of the best.

"Then Toshie and I got on quarrelling about the price of Lachlan Farawa's beasts that he sold at Falkirk; and, the drink having aye a bad effect on my temper, I was for giving him the lie and coming off in a great rage. It was about six o'clock in the evening and an hour to nightfall, so Mistress Craik comes in to try and keep me. 'Losh, Duncan,' says she, 'ye'll never try and win ower the muir the nicht. It's mae than ten mile to Carnwath, and there's nocht atween it and this but whaups and heathery braes.' But when I am roused I will be more obstinate than ten mules, so I would be going, though I knew not under Heaven where I was going till. I was too full of good liquor and good meat to be much worth at thinking, so I got my sheep on the road an' a big bottle in my pouch, and set off into the heather. I knew not what my purpose was, whether I thought to reach the shieling of Carnwath, or whether I expected some house of entertainment to spring up by the wayside. But my fool's mind was set on my purpose of getting some miles further in my journey ere the coming of darkness.

"For some time I jogged happily on, with my sheep running well before me and my dogs trotting at my heels. We left the trees behind and struck out on the broad grassy path which bands the moor like the waist-strap of a sword. It was most dreary and lonesome with never a house in view, only bogs and grey hillsides, and ill-looking waters. It was stony, too, and this more than aught else caused my Dutch courage to fail me, for I soon fell wearied, since much whisky is bad travelling fare, and began to curse my folly. Had my pride no kept me back, I would have returned to Lucky Craik's; but I was like the devil for stiffneckedness, and thought of nothing but to push on.

"I own that I was verra well tired and quite spiritless when I first saw the House. I had scarce been an hour on the way, and the light was not quite gone; but still it was geyan dark, and the place sprang somewhat suddenly on my sight. For, looking a little to the left, I saw over a little strip of grass a big square dwelling with many outhouses, half farm and half pleasure-house. This, I thought, is the verra place I have been seeking and made sure of finding, so whistling a gay tune, I drove my flock toward it.

"When I came to the gate of the court, I saw better of what sort was the building I had arrived at. There was a square yard with monstrous high walls, at the left of which was the main block of the house, and on the right what I took to be the byres and stables. The place looked ancient, and the stone in many places was crumbling away; but the style was of yesterday, and in no way differing from that of a hundred steadings in the land. There were some kind of arms above the gateway, and a bit of an iron stanchion; and when I had my sheep inside of it, I saw that the court was all grown up with green grass. And what seemed queer in that dusky half-light was the want of sound. There was no neichering of horses, nor routing of kye, nor clack of hens, but all as still as the top of Ben Cruachan. It was warm and pleasant, too, though the night was chill without.

"I had no sooner entered the place than a row of sheep-pens caught my eye, fixed against the wall in front. This I thought mighty convenient, so I made all haste to put my beasts into them; and finding that there was a good supply of hay within, I left them easy in my mind, and turned about to look for the door of the House.

"To my wonder, when I found it, it was open wide to the wall; so, being confident with much whisky, I never took thought to knock, but walked boldly in. There's some careless folk here, thinks I to myself, and I much misdoubt if the man knows aught about farming. He'll maybe just be a town's body taking the air on the muirs.

"The place I entered upon was a hall, not like a muirland farmhouse, but more fine than I had ever seen. It was laid with a verra fine carpet, all red and blue and gay colours, and in the corner in a fireplace a great fire crackled. There were chairs, too, and a walth of old rusty arms on the walls, and all manner of whigmaleeries that folk think ornamental. But nobody was there, so I made for the staircase which was at the further side, and went up it stoutly. I made scarce any noise, so thickly was it carpeted, and I will own it kind of terrified me to be walking in such a place. But when a man has drunk well he is troubled not overmuckle with modesty or fear, so I e'en stepped out and soon came to a landing where was a door.

"Now, thinks I, at last I have won to the habitable parts of the house; so laying my finger on the sneck I lifted it and entered, and there before me was the finest room in all the world; indeed I abate not a jot of the phrase, for I cannot think of anything finer. It was hung with braw pictures and lined with big bookcases of oak well-filled with books in fine bindings. The furnishing seemed carved by a skilled hand, and the cushions and curtains were soft velvet. But the best thing was the table, which was covered with a clean white cloth and set with all kind of good meat and drink. The dishes were of silver, and as bright as Loch Awe water in an April sun. Eh, but it was a braw, braw sight for a drover! And there at the far end, with a great bottle of wine before him, sat the master.

"He rose as I entered, and I saw him to be dressed in the best of town fashion, a man of maybe fifty years, but hale and well-looking, with a peaked beard and trimmed moustache and thick eyebrows. His eyes were slanted a thought, which is a thing I hate in any man, but his whole appearance was pleasing.

" 'Mr Stewart?' says he courteously, looking at me. 'Is it Mr Duncan Stewart that I will be indebted to for the honour of this visit?'

"I stared at him blankly, for how did he ken my name?

" 'That is my name,' I said, 'but who the tevil tell 't you about it?'

" 'Oh, my name is Stewart myself,' says he, 'and all Stewarts should be well acquaint.'

" 'True,' said I, 'though I don't mind your face before. But now I am here, I think you have a most gallant place, Mr Stewart.'

" 'Well enough. But how have you come to 't? We've few visitors.'

"So I told him where I had come from, and where I was going, and why I was forewandered at this time of night among the muirs. He listened keenly, and when I had finished, he says verra friendly-like, 'Then you'll bide all night and take supper with me. It would never be doing to let one of the clan go away without breaking bread. Sit ye down, Mr Duncan.'

"I sat down gladly enough, though I own that at first I did not half like the whole business. There was something unchristian about the place, and for certain it was not seemly that the man's name should be the same as my own, and that he should be so well posted in my doings. But he seemed so well-disposed that my misgivings soon vanished.

"So I seated myself at the table opposite my entertainer. There was a place laid ready for me, and beside the knife and fork a long horn-handled spoon. I had never seen a spoon so long and queer, and I asked the man what it meant. 'Oh,' says he, 'the broth in this house is very often hot, so we need a long spoon to sup it. It is a common enough thing, is it not?'

"I could answer nothing to this, though it did not seem to me sense, and I had an inkling of something I had heard about long spoons which I thought was not good; but my wits were not clear, as I have told you already. A serving man brought me a great bowl of soup and set it before me. I had hardly plunged spoon intil it, when Mr Stewart cries out from the other end: 'Now, Mr Duncan, I call you to witness that you sit down to supper of your own accord. I've an ill name in these parts for compelling folk to take meat with me when they dinna want it. But you'll bear me witness that you're willing.'

" 'Yes, by God, I am that,' I said, for the savoury smell of the broth was rising to my nostrils. The other smiled at this as if well-pleased.

"I have tasted many soups, but I swear there never was one like that. It was as if all the good things in the world were mixed thegether – whisky and kale and shortbread and cocky-leeky and honey and salmon. The taste of it was enough to make a body's heart loup with fair gratitude. The smell of it was like the spicy winds of Arabia, that you read about in the Bible, and when you had taken a spoonful you felt as happy as if you had sellt a hundred yowes at twice their reasonable worth. Oh, it was grand soup!

" 'What Stewarts did you say you comed from?' I asked my entertainer.

" 'Oh,' he says, 'I'm connected with them all, Athole Stewarts, Appin Stewarts, Rannoch Stewarts, and a'. I've a heap o' land thereaways.'

" 'Whereabouts?' says I, wondering. 'Is 't at the Blair o' Athole, or along by Tummel side, or wast the Loch o' Rannoch, or on the Muir, or in Benderloch?'

" 'In all the places you name,' says he.

" 'Got damn,' says I, 'then what for do you not bide there instead of in these stinking law-lands?'

"At this he laughed softly to himself. 'Why, for maybe the same reason as yoursel, Mr Duncan. You know the proverb, "A' Stewarts are sib to the Deil." '

"I laughed loudly, 'Oh, you've been a wild one, too, have you? Then you're not worse than mysel. I ken the inside of every public in the Cowgate and Cannongate, and there's no another drover on the road my match at fechting and drinking and dicing.' And I started on a long shameless catalogue of my misdeeds. Mr Stewart meantime listened with a satisfied smirk on his face.

" 'Yes, I've heard tell of you, Mr Duncan,' he says. 'But here's something more, and you'll doubtless be hungry.'

"And now there was set on the table a round of beef garnished with pot-herbs, all most delicately fine to the taste. From a great cupboard were brought many bottles of wine, and in a massive silver bowl at the table's head were put whisky and lemons and sugar. I do not know well what I drank, but whatever it might be it was the best ever brewed. It made you scarce feel the earth round about you, and you were so happy you could scarce keep from singing. I wad give much siller to this day for the receipt.

"Now, the wine made me talk, and I began to boast of my own great qualities, the things I had done and the things I was going to do. I was a drover just now, but it was not long that I would be being a drover. I had bought a flock of my own, and would sell it for a hundred pounds, no less; with that I would buy a bigger one till I had made money enough to stock a farm; and then I would leave the road and spend my days in peace, seeing to my land and living in good company. Was not my father, I cried, own cousin, thrice removed, to Maclean o' Duart, and my mother's uncle's wife a Rory of Balnacrory? And I am a scholar too, said I, for I was a matter of two years at Embro' College, and might have been roaring in the pulpit, if I hadna liked the drink and the lasses too well.

" 'See,' said I, 'I will prove it to you'; and I rose from the table and went to one of the bookcases. There were all manner of books, Latin and Greek, poets and philosophers, but in the main, divinity. For there I saw Richard Baxter's 'Call to the Unconverted', and Thomas Boston of Ettrick's 'Fourfold State', not to speak of the *Sermons* of half a hundred auld ministers, and the 'Hind let Loose', and many books of the covenanting folk.

" 'Faith,' I says, 'you've a fine collection, Mr What's-your-name,' for the wine had made me free in my talk. 'There is many a minister and professor in the Kirk, I'll warrant, who has a less godly library. I begin to suspect you of piety, sir.'

" 'Does it not behove us,' he answered in an unctuous voice, 'to mind the words of Holy Writ that evil communications corrupt good manners, and have an eye to our company? These are all the company I have, except when some stranger such as you honours me with a visit.'

"I had meantime been opening a book of plays, I think by the famous William Shakespeare, and I here broke into a loud laugh. 'Ha, ha, Mr Stewart,' I says, 'here's a sentence I've lighted on which is hard on you. Listen! "The Devil can quote Scripture to advantage." '

"The other laughed long. 'He who wrote that was a shrewd man,' he said, 'but I'll warrant if you'll open another volume, you'll find some quip on yourself.'

"I did as I was bidden, and picked up a white-backed book, and opening it at random, read: 'There be many who spend their days in evil and wine-bibbing, in lusting and cheating, who think to mend while yet there is time; but the opportunity is to them for ever awanting, and they go down openmouthed to the great fire.'

" 'Psa,' I cried, 'some wretched preaching book, I will have none of them. Good wine will be better than bad theology.' So I sat down once more at the table.

" 'You're a clever man, Mr Duncan,' he says, 'and a well-read one. I commend your spirit in breaking away from the bands of the kirk and the college, though your father was so thrawn against you.'

" 'Enough of that,' I said, 'though I don't know who telled you.' I was angry to hear my father spoken of, as though the grieving him was a thing to be proud of.

" 'Oh, as you please,' he says; 'I was just going to say that I commended your spirit in sticking the knife into the man in the Pleasaunce, the time you had to hide for a month about the backs o' Leith.'

" 'How do you ken that?' I asked hotly. 'You've heard more about me than ought to be repeated, let me tell you.'

" 'Don't be angry,' he said sweetly; 'I like you well for these things, and you mind the lassie in Athole that was so fond of you. You treated her well, did you not?'

"I made no answer, being too much surprised at his knowledge of things which I thought none knew but myself.

" 'Oh, yes, Mr Duncan. I could tell you what you were doing today, how you cheated Jock Gallowa out of six pounds, and sold a horse to the farmer of Haypath that was scarce fit to carry him home. And I know what you are meaning to do the morn at Glesca, and I wish you well of it.'

" 'I think you must be the Devil,' I said blankly.

" 'The same, at your service,' said he, still smiling.

"I looked at him in terror, and even as I looked I kenned by something in his eyes and the twitch of his lips that he was speaking the truth.

" 'And what place is this, you…' I stammered.

" 'Call me Mr S,' he says gently, 'and enjoy your stay while you are here and don't concern yourself about the lawing.'

" 'The lawing!' I cried in astonishment, 'and is this a house of public entertainment?'

" 'To be sure, else how is a poor man to live?'

" 'Name it,' said I, 'and I will pay and be gone.'

" 'Well,' said he, 'I make it a habit to give a man his choice. In your case it will be your wealth or your chances hereafter, in plain English your flock or your – '

" 'My immortal soul,' I gasped.

" 'Your soul,' said Mr S, bowing, 'though I think you call it by too flattering an adjective.'

" 'You damned thief,' I roared, 'you would entice a man into your accursed house and then strip him bare!'

" 'Hold hard,' said he, 'don't let us spoil our good fellowship by incivilities. And, mind you, I took you to witness to begin with that you sat down of your own accord.'

" 'So you did,' said I, and could say no more.

" 'Come, come,' he says, 'don't take it so bad. You may keep all your gear and yet part from here in safety. You've but to sign your name, which is no hard task to a college-bred man, and go on living as you live just now to the end. And let me tell you, Mr Duncan Stewart, that you should take it as a great obligement that I am willing to take your bit soul instead of fifty sheep. There's no many would value it so high.'

" 'Maybe no, maybe no,' I said sadly, 'but it's all I have. D'ye no see that if I gave it up, there would be no chance left of mending? And I'm sure I do not want your company to all eternity.'

" 'Faith, that's uncivil,' he says; 'I was just about to say that we had had a very pleasant evening.'

"I sat back in my chair very downhearted; I must leave this place as poor as a kirk-mouse, and begin again with little but the clothes on my back. I was strongly tempted to sign the bit paper thing and have done with it all, but somehow I could not bring myself to do it. So at last I says to him: 'Well, I've made up my mind. I'll give you my sheep, sorry though I be to lose them, and I hope I may never come near this place again as long as I live.'

" 'On the contrary,' he said, 'I hope often to have the pleasure of your company. And seeing that you've paid well for your lodging, I hope you'll make the best of them. Don't be sparing on the drink.'

"I looked hard at him for a second. 'You've an ill name, and an ill trade, but you're no a bad sort yoursel, and, do you ken, I like you.'

" 'I'm much obliged to you for the character,' says he, 'and I'll take your hand on 't.'

"So I filled up my glass and we set to, and such an evening I never mind of. We never got fou, but just in a fine good temper and very entertaining. The stories we told and the jokes we cracked are still a kind of memory with me, though I could not come over one of them. And then, when I got sleepy, I was shown to the brawest bedroom, all hung with pictures and looking-glasses, and with bedclothes of the finest linen and a coverlet of silk. I bade Mr S goodnight, and my head was scarce on the pillow ere I was sound asleep.

"When I awoke the sun was just newly risen, and the frost of a September morning was on my clothes. I was lying among green braes with nothing near me but crying whaups and heathery hills, and my two dogs running round about and howling as they were mad."

AT THE RISING OF THE WATERS

In mid-September the moors are changing from red to a dusky brown, as the fire of the heather wanes, and the long grass yellows with advancing autumn. Then, too, the rain falls heavily on the hills, and vexes the shallow upland streams, till every glen is ribbed with its churning torrent. This for the uplands; but below, at the rim of the plains, where the glens expand to vales, and trim fields edge the wastes, there is wreck and lamentation. The cabined waters lip over cornland and meadow, and bear destruction to crop and cattle.

This is the tale of Robert Linklater, farmer in Clachlands, and the events which befell him on the night of September 20th, in the year of grace 1880. I am aware that there are characters in the countryside which stand higher in repute than his, for imagination and a love of point and completeness in a story are qualities which little commend themselves to the prosaic. I have heard him called "Leein' Rob", and answer to the same with cheerfulness; but he was wont in private to brag of minutest truthfulness, and attribute his ill name to the universal dullness of man.

On this evening he came home, by his own account, from market about the hour of six. He had had a week of festivity. On the Monday he had gone to a distant cattle show, and on Tuesday to a marriage. On the Wednesday he had attended upon a cousin's funeral, and, being flown with whisky, brought everlasting disgrace upon himself by rising to propose the health of the bride and bridegroom. On Thursday he had been at the market of Gledsmuir,

53

and, getting two shillings more for his ewes than he had reckoned, returned in a fine fervour of spirit and ripe hilarity.

The weather had been shower and blast for days. The grey skies dissolved in dreary rain, and on that very morn there had come a downpour so fierce that the highways ran like a hillside torrent. Now, as he sat at supper and looked down at the green vale and red waters leaping by bank and brae, a sudden fear came to his heart. Hitherto he had had no concern – for was not his harvest safely inned? But now he minds of the laigh parks and the nowt beasts there, which he had bought the week before at the sale of Inverforth. They were Kyloe and Galloway mixed, and on them, when fattened through winter and spring, lay great hopes of profit. He gulped his meal down hurriedly, and went forthwith to the garden foot. There he saw something that did not allay his fears. Gled had split itself in two, at the place where Clachlands water came to swell its flow, and a long, gleaming line of black current stole round by the side of the laigh meadow, where stood the huddled cattle. Let but the waters rise a little, and the valley would be one uniform, turgid sea.

This was pleasing news for an honest man after a hard day's work, and the farmer went grumbling back. He took a mighty plaid and flung it over his shoulders, chose the largest and toughest of his many sticks, and set off to see wherein he could better the peril.

Now, some hundreds of yards above the laigh meadow, a crazy wooden bridge spanned the stream. By this way he might bring his beasts to safety, for no nowt could hope to swim the red flood. So he plashed through the dripping stubble to the river's brink, where, with tawny swirl, it licked the edge of banks which in summer weather stood high and flower-decked. Ruefully he reflected that many good palings would by this time be whirling to a distant sea.

When he came to the wooden bridge he set his teeth manfully and crossed. It creaked and swayed with his weight, and dipped till it all but touched the flow. It could not stand even as the water was, for already its mid prop had lurched forward, like a drunken man, and was groaning at each wave. But if a rise came, it would be torn from its foundations like a reed, and then heigh-ho! for cattle and man.

With painful haste he laboured through the shallows which rimmed the haughlands, and came to the snakelike current which had even now spread itself beyond the laigh meadow. He measured its depth with his eye and ventured. It did not reach beyond his middle, but its force gave him much ado to keep his feet. At length it was passed, and he stood triumphant on the spongy land, where the cattle huddled in mute discomfort and terror.

Darkness was falling, and he could scarcely see the homestead on the affronting hillside. So with all speed he set about collecting the shivering beasts, and forcing them through the ring of water to the bridge. Up to their flanks they went, and then stood lowing helplessly. He saw that something was wrong, and made to ford the current himself. But now it was beyond him. He looked down at the yellow water running round his middle, and saw that it had risen, and was rising inch by inch with every minute. Then he glanced to where aforetime stood the crazy planking of the bridge. Suddenly hope and complacency fled, and the gravest fear settled in his heart; for he saw no bridge, only a ragged, sawlike end of timber where once he had crossed.

Here was a plight for a solitary man to be in at nightfall. There would be no wooden bridge on all the water, and the nearest one of stone was at distant Gledsmuir, over some score of miles of weary moorland. It was clear that his cattle must bide on this farther bank, and he himself, when once he had seen them in safety, would set off for the nearest farm and pass the night. It seemed the craziest of matters, that he should be thus in peril and discomfort, with the lights of his house blinking not a quarter mile away.

Once more he tried to break the water-ring and once more he failed. The flood was still rising, and the space of green which showed grey and black beneath a fitful moon was quickly lessening. Before, irritation had been his upper feeling, now terror succeeded. He could not swim a stroke, and if the field were covered he would drown like a cat in a bag. He lifted up his voice and roared with all the strength of his mighty lungs, "Sammle", "Andra", "Jock", "come and help's", till the place rang with echoes. Meantime, with strained eyes he watched the rise of the cruel water, which crept, black and pitiless, over the shadowy grey.

He drove the beasts to a little knoll, which stood somewhat above the meadow, and there they stood, cattle and man, in the fellowship of misfortune. They had been as wild as peat-reek, and had suffered none to approach them, but now with some instinct of peril they stood quietly by his side, turning great billowy foreheads to the surging waste. Upward and nearer came the current, rising with steady gurgling which told of great storms in his hills and roaring torrents in every gorge. Now the sound grew louder and seemed almost at his feet, now it ceased and nought was heard save the dull hum of the main stream pouring its choking floods to the sea. Suddenly his eyes wandered to the lights of his house and the wide slope beyond, and for a second he mused on some alien trifle. Then he was brought to himself with a pull as he looked and saw a line of black water not three feet from the farthest beast. His heart stood still, and with awe he reflected that in half an hour by this rate of rising he would be with his Maker.

For five minutes he waited, scarce daring to look around him, but dreading each instant to feel a cold wave lick his boot. Then he glanced timorously, and to his joy it was scarce an inch higher. It was stopping, and he might yet be safe. With renewed energy he cried out for aid, till the very cattle started at the sound and moved uneasily among themselves.

In a little there came an answering voice across the dark, "Whae's in the laigh meedy?" and it was the voice of the herd of Clachlands, sounding hoarse through the driving of the stream.

"It's me," went back the mournful response.

"And whae are *ye*?" came the sepulchral voice.

"Your ain maister, William Smail, forewandered among water and nowt beast."

For some time there was no reply, since the shepherd was engaged in a severe mental struggle; with the readiness of his class he went straight to the heart of the peril, and mentally reviewed the ways and waters of the land. Then he calmly accepted the hopelessness of it all, and cried loudly through the void –

"There's nae way for 't but juist to bide where ye are. The water's stoppit, and gin mornin' we'll get ye aff. I'll send a laddie down to the Dow Pule to bring up a boat in a cairt. But that's a lang gait, and it'll be a sair job gettin' it up, and I misdoot it'll be daylicht or he comes. But haud up your hert, and we'll get ye oot. Are the beasts a' richt?"

"A' richt, William; but, 'od man! their maister is cauld. Could ye no fling something ower?"

"No, when there's twae hunner yairds o' deep water atween."

"Then, William, ye maun licht a fire, a great muckle roarin' fire, juist fornenst me. It'll cheer me to see the licht o' 't."

The shepherd did as he was bid, and for many minutes the farmer could hear the noise of men heaping wood, in the pauses of wind and through the thicker murmur of the water. Then a glare shot up, and revealed the dusky forms of the four serving-men straining their eyes across the channel. The gleam lit up a yard of water by the other bank, but all midway was inky shadow. It was about eight o'clock, and the moon was just arisen. The air had coldened and a light chill wind rose from the river.

The farmer of Clachlands, standing among shivering and dripping oxen, himself wet to the skin and cold as a stone, with no wrapping save his plaid, and no outlook save a black moving water and a gleam of fire – in such a position, the farmer of Clachlands collected his thoughts and mustered his resolution. His first consideration was the safety of his stock. The effort gave him comfort. His crops were in, and he could lose nothing there; his sheep were far removed from scaith, and his cattle would survive the night with ease, if the water kept its level. With some satisfaction he reflected that the only care he need have in the matter was for his own bodily comfort in an autumn night. This was serious, yet not deadly, for the farmer was a man of many toils and cared little for the rigours of weather. But he would gladly have given the price of a beast for a bottle of whisky to comfort himself in this emergency.

He stood on a knuckle of green land some twenty feet long, with a crowd of cattle pressing around him and a little forest of horns showing faintly. There was warmth in these great shaggy hides if they had not been drenched and icy from long standing. His fingers were soon as numb as his feet, and it was in vain that he stamped on the plashy grass or wrapped his hands in a fold of plaid. There was no doubt in the matter. He was keenly uncomfortable, and the growing chill of night would not mend his condition.

Some ray of comfort was to be got from the sight of the crackling fire. There at least was homely warmth, and light, and ease. With gusto he conjured up all the delights of the past week, the roaring evenings in market alehouse, and the fragrance of good drink and piping food. Necessity sharpened his fancy, and he could almost feel the flavour of tobacco. A sudden hope took him. He clapped hand to pocket and pulled forth pipe and shag. Curse it! He had left his matchbox on the chimney-top in his kitchen, and there was an end to his only chance of comfort.

So in all cold and damp he set himself to pass the night in the midst of that ceaseless swirl of black moss water. Even as he looked at the dancing glimmer of fire, the moon broke forth silent and full, and lit the vale with misty glamour. The great hills, whence came the Gled, shone blue and high with fleecy trails of vapour drifting athwart them. He saw clearly the walls of his dwelling, the light shining: from the window, the struggling fire on the bank, and the dark forms of men. Its transient flashes on the waves were scarce seen in the broad belt of moonshine which girdled the valley. And around him, before and behind, rolled the unending desert waters with that heavy, resolute flow, which one who knows the floods fears a thousandfold more than the boisterous stir of a torrent.

And so he stood till maybe one o'clock of the morning, cold to the bone, and awed by the eternal silence, which choked him, despite the myriad noises of the night. For there are few things more awful than the calm of nature in her madness – the stillness which follows a snow-slip or the monotony of a great flood. By this hour he was falling from his first high confidence. His knees stooped under him, and he was fain to lean upon the beasts at his side. His shoulders ached with the wet, and his eyes grew sore with the sight of yellow glare and remote distance.

From this point I shall tell his tale in his own words, as he has told it me, but stripped of its garnishing and detail. For it were vain to translate Lallan into orthodox speech, when the very salt of the night air clings to the Scots as it did to that queer tale.

"The mune had been lang out," he said, "and I had grown weary o' her blinkin'. I was as cauld as death, and as wat as the sea, no to speak o' haein' the rheumatics in my back. The nowt were glowrin' and glunchin', rubbin' heid to heid, and whiles stampin' on my taes wi' their cloven hooves. But I was mortal glad o' the beasts' company, for I think I wad hae gane daft mysel in that muckle dowie water. Whiles I thocht it was risin', and then my hert stood still; an' whiles fa'in', and then it loupit wi' joy. But it keepit geyan near the bit, and aye as I heard it lip-lappin' I prayed the Lord to keep it whaur it was.

"About half past yin in the mornin', as I saw by my watch, I got sleepy, and but for the nowt steerin', I micht hae drappit aff. Syne I begood to watch the water, and it was rale interestin', for a' sort o' queer things were comin' doun. I could see bits o' brigs and palin's wi'oot end dippin' in the tide, and whiles swirlin' in sae near that I could hae grippit them. Then beasts began to come by, whiles upside doun, whiles soomin' brawly, sheep and stirks frae the farms up the water. I got graund amusement for a wee while watchin' them, and notin' the marks on their necks.

" 'That's Clachlands Mains,' says I, 'and that's Nether Fallo, and the Back o' the Muneraw. Gudesake, sic a spate it maun hae been up the muirs to work siccan a destruction!' I keepit coont o' the stock, and feegured to mysel what the farmer-bodies wad lose. The thocht that I wad keep a' my ain was some kind o' comfort.

"But about the hour o' twae the mune cloudit ower, and I saw nae mair than twenty feet afore me. I got awesome cauld, and a sort o' stound o' fricht took me, as I lookit into that black, unholy water. The nowt shivered sair and drappit their heids, and the fire on the ither side seemed to gang out a' of a sudden, and leave the hale glen thick wi' nicht. I shivered mysel wi' something mair than the snell air, and there and then I wad hae gien the price o' fower stirks for my ain bed at hame.

"It was as quiet as a kirkyaird, for suddenly the roar o' the water stoppit, and the stream lay still as a loch. Then I heard a queer lappin' as o' something floatin' doun, and it sounded miles aff in that dreidfu' silence. I listened wi' een stertin', and aye it cam' nearer and nearer, wi' a sound like a dowg soomin' a burn. It was sae black, I could see nocht, but somewhere frae the edge o' a cloud, a thin ray o' licht drappit on the water, and there, soomin' doun by me, I saw something that lookit like a man.

"My hert was burstin' wi' terror, but, thinks I, here's a droonin' body, and I maun try and save it. So I waded in as far as I daured, though my feet were sae cauld that they bowed aneath me.

"Ahint me I heard a splashin' and fechtin', and then I saw the nowt, fair wild wi' fricht, standin' in the water on the ither side o' the green bit, and lookin' wi' muckle feared een at something in the water afore me.

"Doun the thing came, and aye I got caulder as I looked. Then it was by my side, and I claught at it and pu'd it after me on to the land.

"I heard anither splash. The nowt gaed farther into the water, and stood shakin' like young birks in a storm.

"I got the thing upon the green bank and turned it ower. It was a drooned man wi' his hair hingin' back on his broo, and his mouth wide open. But first I saw his een, which glowered like scrapit lead out o' his clay-cauld face, and had in them a' the fear o' death and hell which follows after.

"The next moment I was up to my waist among the nowt, fechtin' in the water aside them, and snowkin' into their wet backs to hide mysel like a feared bairn.

"Maybe half an 'oor I stood, and then my mind returned to me. I misca'ed mysel for a fule and a coward. And my legs were sae numb, and my strength sae far gane, that I kenned fine that I couldna lang thole to stand this way like a heron in the water.

"I lookit round, and then turned again wi' a stert, for there were thae leaden een o' that awfu' deid thing staring at me still.

"For anither quarter-hour I stood and shivered, and then my guid sense returned, and I tried again. I walkit backward, never lookin' round, through the water to the shore, whaur I thocht the corp was lyin'. And a' the time I could hear my hert chokin' in my breist.

"My God, I fell ower it, and for one moment lay aside it, wi' my heid touchin' its deathly skin. Then wi' a skelloch like a daft man, I took the thing in my airms and flung it wi' a' my strength into the water. The swirl took it, and it dipped and swam like a fish till it gaed out o' sicht.

"I sat doun on the grass and grat like a bairn wi' fair horror and weakness. Yin by yin the nowt came back, and shouthered anither around me, and the puir beasts brocht me yince mair to mysel. But I keepit my een on the grund, and thocht o' hame and a' thing decent and kindly, for I daurna for my life look out to the black water in dreid o' what it micht bring.

"At the first licht, the herd and twae ither men cam' ower in a boat to tak me aff and bring fodder for the beasts. They fand me still sitting wi' my heid atween my knees, and my face like a peeled wand. They lifted me intil the boat and rowed me ower, driftin' far down wi' the angry current. At the ither side the shepherd says to me in an awed voice –

" 'There's a fearfu' thing happened. The young laird o' Manorwater's drooned in the spate. He was ridin' back late and tried the ford o' the Cauldshaw foot. Ye ken his wild cantrips, but there's an end o' them noo. The horse cam' hame in the nicht wi' an empty saiddle, and the Gled Water rinnin' frae him in streams. The corp'll be far on to the sea by this time, and they'll never see 't mair.'

" 'I ken,' I cried wi' a dry throat, 'I ken; I saw him floatin' by.' And then I broke yince mair into a silly greetin', while the men watched me as if they thocht I was out o' my mind."

So much the farmer of Clachlands told me, but to the countryside he repeated merely the bare facts of weariness and discomfort. I have heard that he was accosted a week later by the minister of the place, a well-intentioned, phrasing man, who had strayed from his native city with its familiar air of tea and temperance to those stony uplands.

"And what thoughts had you, Mr Linklater, in that awful position? Had you no serious reflection upon your life?"

"Me," said the farmer; "no me. I juist was thinkin' that it was dooms cauld, and that I wad hae gien a guid deal for a pipe o' tobaccy." This in the racy, careless tone of one to whom such incidents were the merest child's play.

THE EARLIER AFFECTION

My host accompanied me to the foot of the fine avenue which looks from Portnacroish to the steely sea-loch. The smoke of the clachan was clear in the air, and the morn was sweet with young leaves and fresh salt breezes. For all about us were woods, till the moor dipped to the water, and then came the great shining spaces straight to the edge of Morven and the stony Ardgower Hills.

"You will understand, Mr Townshend," said my entertainer, "that I do not fall in with your errand. It is meet that youth should be wild, but you had been better playing your pranks about Oxford than risking your neck on our Hieland hills, and this but two year come Whitsuntide since the late grievous troubles. It had been better to forget your mother and give your Cameron kin the go-by, than run your craig into the same tow as Ewan's by seeking him on Brae Mamore. Stewart though I be, and proud of my name, I would think twice before I set out on such a ploy. It's likely that Ewan will be blithe to see you and no less to get your guineas, but there are easier ways of helping a friend than just to go to his hidey-hole."

But I would have none of Mr Stewart's arguments, for my heart was hot on this fool's journey. My cousin Ewan was in the heather, with his head well-priced by his enemies and his friends dead or broken. I was little more than a boy let loose from college, and it seemed paradise itself to thus adventure my person among the wilds.

"Then if you will no take an old man's telling, here's a word for you to keep mind of on the road. There are more that have a grudge against the Cameron than King George's soldiers. Be sure there will be pickings going up Lochaber-ways, and all the Glasgow pack-men and low-country trading-bodies that have ever had their knife in Lochiel will be down on the broken house like a pack of kites. It's not impossible that ye may meet a wheen on the road, for I heard news of some going north from the Campbell country, and it bodes ill for any honest gentleman who may foregather with the black clan. Forbye, there'll be them that will come from Glenurchy-side and Breadalbin, so see you keep a quiet tongue and a watchful eye if ye happen on strangers."

And with this last word I had shaken his hand, turned my horse to the north, and ridden out among the trees.

The sound of sea water was ever in my ears, for the road twined in the links of coast and crooks of hill, now dipping to the tide's edge, and now rising to a great altitude amid the heather. The morn was so fresh and shining that I fell in love with myself and my errand, and when I turned a corner and saw a wall of blue hill rise gleaming to the heavens with snow-filled corries, I cried out for the fair land I had come to, and my fine adventure.

By the time I came to Duror it was midday, and I stopped for refreshment. There is an inn in Duror, where cheese and bread and usquebagh were to be had – fare enough for a hungry traveller. But when I was on the road again, as I turned the crook of hill by the Heugh of Ardsheal, lo! I was in the thick of a party of men.

They were five in all, dressed soberly in black and brown and grey, and riding the soberest of beasts. Mr Stewart's word rose in my memory, and I shut my mouth and composed my face to secrecy. They would not trouble me long, this covey of merchant-folk, for they would get the ferry at Ballachulish, which was not my road to Brae Mamore.

So I gave them a civil greeting, and would have ridden by, had not Fate stepped in my way. My horse shied at a stick by the roadside, and ere I knew I was jostling and scattering them, trying to curb the accursed tricks of my beast.

After this there was nothing for it but to apologise, and what with my hurry and chagrin I was profuse enough. They looked at me with startled eyes, and one had drawn a pistol from his holster, but when they found I was no reiver they took the thing in decent part.

"It's a sma' maitter," said one with a thick burr in his voice. "The hert o' a man and the hoofs o' a horse are controlled by nane but our Makker, as my faither aye said. Ye're no to blame, young sir."

I fell into line with the odd man – for they rode in pairs, and in common civility I could not push on through them. As I rode behind I had leisure to look at my company. All were elderly men, their ages lying perhaps between five and thirty and twoscore, and all rode with the air of townsmen out on a holiday. They talked gravely among themselves, now looking at the sky (which was clouding over, as is the fashion in a Highland April), and now casting inquiring glances towards my place at the back. The man with whom I rode was a little fellow, younger than the rest and more ruddy and frank of face. He was willing to talk, which he did in a very vile Scots accent which I had hard work to follow. His name he said was Macneil, but he knew nothing of the Highlands, for his abode was Paisley. He questioned me of myself with some curiosity.

"Oh, my name is Townshend," said I, speaking the truth at random, "and I have come up from England to see if the report of your mountains be true. It is a better way of seeing the world, say I, than to philander through Italy and France. I am a quiet man of modest means with a taste for the picturesque."

"So, so," said the little man. "But I could show you corn-rigs by the Cart side which are better and bonnier than a wheen muckle stony hills. But every man to his taste, and doubtless, since ye're an Englander, ye'll no hae seen mony brae-faces?"

Then he fell to giving me biographies of each of the travellers, and as we were some way behind the others he could speak without fear. "The lang man in the grey coat is the Deacon o' the Glesca Fleshers, a man o' great substance and good repute. He's lang had trouble wi' thae Hieland bodies, for when he bocht nowt frae them they wad seek a loan of maybe mair than the price, and he wad get caution on some o' their lands and cot-houses. 'Deed, we're a' in that line, as ye micht say;" and he raked the horizon with his hand.

"Then ye go north to recover monies?" said I, inadvertently.

He looked cunningly into my face, and for a second, suspicion was large in his eyes. "Ye're a gleg yin, Mr Townds, and maybe our errand is just no that far frae what ye mean. But, speaking o' the Deacon, he has a grand-gaun business in the Trongate, and he has been elder this sax year in the Barony, and him no forty year auld. Laidly's his name, and nane mair respeckit among the merchants o' the city. Yon ither man wi' him is a Maister Graham, whae comes frae the Menteith way, a kind o' Hielander by bluid, but wi' nae Hieland tricks in his heid. He's a sober wud-merchant at the Broomielaw, and he has come up here on a job about some fir-wuds. Losh, there's a walth o' timmer in this bit," and he scanned greedily the shady hills.

"The twae lang red-heided men are Campbells, brithers, whae deal in yairn and wabs o' a' kind in the Saltmarket. Gin ye were wantin' the guid hamespun or the fine tartan in a' the clan colours ye wad be wise to gang there. But I'm forgetting ye dinna belang to thae pairts ava'."

By this time the heavens had darkened to a storm and the great raindrops were already plashing on my face. We were now round the ribs of the hill they call Sgordhonuill and close to the edge of the Levin loch. It was a desolate, wild place, and yet on the very brink of the shore amid the birk-woods we came on the inn and the ferry.

I must needs go in with the others, and if the place was better than certain hostels I had lodged in on my road – notably in the accursed land of Lorne – it was far short of the South. And yet I dare not deny the comfort, for there was a peat fire glowing on the hearth and the odour of cooking meat was rich for hungry nostrils. Forbye, the out of doors was now one pour of hail-water, which darkened the evening to a murky twilight.

The men sat round the glow after supper and there was no more talk of going further. The loch was a chaos of white billows, so the ferry was out of the question; and as for me, who should have been that night on Glen Levin-side, there was never a thought of stirring in my head, but I fell into a deep contentment with the warmth and a full meal, and never cast a look to the blurred window. I had not yet spoken to the others, but comfort loosened their tongues, and soon we were all on terms of gossip. They set themselves to find out every point in my career and my intentions, and I, mindful of Mr Stewart's warning, grew as austere in manner as the Deacon himself.

"And ye say ye traivel to see the world?" said one of the Campbells. "Man, ye've little to dae. Ye maunna be thrang at hame. If I had a son who was a drone like you, he wad never finger siller o' mine."

"But I will shortly have a trade," said I, "for I shall be cutting French throats in a year, Mr Campbell, if luck favours me."

"Hear to him," said the grave Campbell. "He talks of war, bloody war, as a man wad talk of a penny-wedding. Know well, young man, that I value a sodger's trade lower than a flesher-lad's, and have no respect for a bright sword and a red coat. I am for peace, but when I speak, for battle they are strong," said he, finishing with a line from one of his Psalms.

I sat rebuked, wishing myself well rid of this company. But I was not to be let alone, for the Deacon would play the inquisitor on the matter of my family.

"What brought ye here of a' places? There are mony pairts in the Hielands better worth seeing. Ye'll hae some freends, belike, hereaways."

I told him, "No," that I had few friends above the Border; but the persistent man would not be pacified. He took upon himself, as the elder, to admonish me on the faults of youth.

"Ye are but a lad," said he with unction, "and I wad see no ill come to ye. But the Hielands are an unsafe bit, given up to malignants and papists and black cattle. Tak your ways back, and tell your freends to thank the Lord that they see ye again." And then he broke into a most violent abuse of the whole place, notably the parts of Appin and Lochaber. It was, he said, the last refuge of all that was vicious and wasteful in the land.

"It is at least a place of some beauty," I broke in with.

"Beauty," he cried scornfully, "d' ye see beauty in black rocks and a grummly sea? Gie me the lown fields about Lanerick, and a' the kind canty south country, and I wad let your bens and corries alane."

And then Graham launched forth in a denunciation of the people. It was strange to hear one who bore his race writ large in his name talk of the inhabitants of these parts as liars and thieves and good-for-nothings. "What have your Hielands done," he cried, "for the well-being of this land? They stir up rebellions wi' papists and the French, and harry the lands o' the god-fearing. They look down on us merchants, and turn up their hungry noses at decent men, as if cheatry were mair gentrice than honest wark. God, I wad have the lot o' them shipped to the Indies and set to learn a decent living."

I sat still during the torrent, raging at the dull company I had fallen in with, for I was hot with youth and had little admiration for the decencies. Then the Deacon, taking a Bible from his valise, declared his intention of conducting private worship ere we retired to rest. It was a ceremony I had never dreamed of before, and in truth I cannot fancy a stranger. First the company sang a psalm with vast unction and no melody. Then the Deacon

68

read from some prophet or other, and finally we were all on our knees while a Campbell offered up a prayer.

After that there was no thought of sitting longer, for it seemed that it was the rule of these people to make their prayers the last article in the day. They lay and snored in their comfortless beds, while I, who preferred the safety of a chair to the unknown dangers of such bedding, dozed uneasily before the peats till the grey April morning.

Dawn came in with a tempest, and when the household was stirring and we had broken our fast, a storm from the north-west was all but tearing the roof from above our heads. Without, the loch was a chasm of mist and white foam, and waves broke hoarsely over the shore road. The landlord, who was also the ferryman, ran about, crying the impossibility of travel. No boat could live a moment in that water, and unless our honours would go round the loch head into Mamore there was nothing for it but to kick our heels in the public.

The merchants conferred darkly among themselves, and there was much shaking of heads. Then the Deacon came up to me with a long face.

"There's nothing for 't," said he, "but to risk the loch head and try Wade's road to Fort William. I dinna mind if that was to be your way, Mr Townds, but it maun be ours, for our business winna wait; so if you're so inclined, we'll be glad o' your company."

Heaven knows I had no further desire for theirs, but I dared not evade. Once in the heart of Brae Mamore I would find means to give them the slip and find the herd's shieling I had been apprised of, where I might get shelter and news of Ewan. I accepted with as cordial a tone as I could muster, and we set out into the blinding weather.

The road runs up the loch by the clachan of Ballachulish, fords the small stream of Coe which runs down from monstrous precipices, and then, winding round the base of the hill they call Pap of Glencoe, comes fairly into Glen Levin. A more desert place

I have not seen. On all sides rose scarred and ragged hills; below, the loch gleamed dully like lead; and the howling storm shook the lone fir trees and dazed our eyes with wrack. The merchants pulled their cloak capes over their heads and set themselves manfully to the toil, but it was clearly not to their stomach, for they said scarcely a word to themselves or me. Only Macneil kept a good temper, but his words were whistled away into the wind.

All the way along that dreary brae-face we were slipping and stumbling cruelly. The men had poor skill in guiding a horse, for though they were all well-grown fellows they had the look of those who are better used to bare-leg rough-foot walking than to stirrup and saddle. Once I had to catch the Deacon's rein and pull him up on the path, or without doubt he would soon have been feeding the ravens at the foot of Corrynakeigh. He thanked me with a grumble, and I saw how tight-drawn were his lips and eyebrows. The mist seemed to get into my brain, and I wandered befogged and foolish in this unknown land. It was the most fantastic misery: underfoot wet rock and heather, on all sides grey dripping veils of rain, and no sound to cheer save a hawk's scream or the crying of an old blackcock from the height, while down in the glen bottom there was the hoarse roaring of torrents.

And then all of a sudden from the darkness there sprang out a gleam of scarlet, and we had stumbled on a party of soldiers. Some twenty in all, they were marching slowly down the valley, and at the sight of us they grew at once alert. We were seized and questioned till they had assured themselves of our credentials. The merchants they let go at once, but I seemed to stick in their throat.

"What are you after, sir, wandering at such a season north of the Highland line?" the captain of them kept asking.

When I told him my tale of seeking the picturesque he would not believe it, till I lost all patience under the treatment.

"Confound it, sir," I cried, "is my speech like that of a renegade Scots Jacobite? I thought my English tongue sufficient surety. And if you ask for a better you have but to find some decent military headquarters where they will tell you that Arthur Townshend is gazetted ensign in the King's own regiment and will proceed within six months to service abroad."

When I had talked him over, the man made an apology of a sort, but he still looked dissatisfied. Then he turned roundly on us. "Do you know young Fassiefern?" he asked.

My companions disclaimed any knowledge save by repute, and even I had the grace to lie stoutly.

"If I thought you were friends of Ewan Cameron," said he, "you should go no further. It's well known that he lies in hiding in these hills, and this day he is to be routed out and sent to the place he deserves. If you meet a dark man of the middle size with two-three ragged Highlanders at his back, you will know that you have foregathered with Ewan Cameron and that King George's men will not be far behind him."

Then the Deacon unloosed the bands of his tongue and spoke a homily. "What have I to dae," he cried, "with the graceless breed of the Camerons? If I saw this Ewan of Fassiefern on the bent then I wad be as hot to pursue him as any redcoat. Have I no suffered from him and his clan, and wad I no gladly see every yin o' them clapped in the Tolbooth?" And with the word he turned to a Campbell for approval and received a fierce nod of his red head.

"I must let you pass, sirs," said the captain, "but if you would keep out of harm's way you will go back to the Levin shore. Ewan's days of freedom are past, and he will be hemmed in by my men here and a like party from Fort William in front, and outflanked on both sides by other companies. I speak to you as honest gentlemen, and I bid you keep a good watch for the Cameron, if you would be in good grace with the King." And without more ado he bade his men march.

Our company after this meeting was very glum for a mile or two. The Deacon's ire had been roused by the hint of suspicion, and he grumbled to himself till his anger found vent in a free cursing of the whole neighbourhood and its people. "Deil take them," he cried, "and shame that I should say it, but it's a queer bit where an honest man canna gang his ways without a red-coated sodger casting een at him." And Graham joined his plaint, till the whole gang lamented like a tinker's funeral.

It was now about midday, and the weather, if aught, had grown fiercer. The mist was clearing, but blasts of chill snow drove down on our ears, and the strait pass before us was grey with the fall. In front lay the sheer mountains, the tangle of loch and broken rocks where Ewan lay hid, and into the wilderness ran our bridle path. Somewhere on the hillsides were sentries, somewhere on the road before us was a troop of soldiers, and between them my poor cousin was fairly enclosed. I felt a sort of madness in my brain, as I thought of his fate. Here was I in the company of Whig traders, with no power to warn him, but going forward to see his capture.

A desperate thought struck me, and I slipped from my horse and made to rush into the bowels of the glen. Once there I might climb unseen up the pass, and get far enough in advance to warn him of his danger. My seeing him would be the wildest chance, yet I might take it. But as I left the path I caught a tree root and felt my heels dangle in the void. That way lay sheer precipice. With a quaking heart I pulled myself up, and made my excuse of an accident as best I could to my staring companions.

Yet the whole pass was traversed without a sight of a human being. I watched every moment to see the troop of redcoats with Ewan in their grip. But no redcoats came; only fresh gusts of snow and the same dreary ribs of hill. Soon we had left the pass and were out on a windy neck of mountain where hags and lochans gloomed among the heather.

And then suddenly as if from the earth there sprang up three men. Even in the mist I saw the red Cameron tartan, and my heart leapt to my mouth. Two were great stalwart men, their clothes drenched and ragged, and the rust on their weapons. But the third was clearly the gentleman – of the middle size, slim, dressed well though also in some raggedness. At the sight the six of us stopped short and gazed dumbly at the three on the path.

I rushed forward and gripped my cousin's hand. "Ewan," I cried, "I am your cousin Townshend come north to put his back to yours. Thank God you are still unharmed;" and what with weariness and anxiety I had almost wept on his neck.

At my first step my cousin had raised his pistol, but when he saw my friendliness he put it back in his belt. When he heard of my cousinship his eyes shone with kindliness, and he bade me welcome to his own sorry country. "My dear cousin," he said, "you have found me in a perilous case and ill-fitted to play the host. But I bid you welcome for a most honest gentleman and kinsman to these few acres of heather that are all now left to me."

And then before the gaping faces of my comrades I stammered out my story. "Oh, Ewan, there's death before and behind you and on all sides. There's a troop waiting down the road and there are dragoons coming at your back. You cannot escape, and these men with me are Whigs and Glasgow traders, and no friends to the Cameron name."

The three men straightened themselves like startled deer.

"How many passed you?" cried Ewan.

"Maybe a score," said I.

He stopped for a while in deep thought.

"Then there's not above a dozen behind me. There are four of us here, true men, and five who are no. We must go back or forward, for a goat could not climb these craigs. Well-a-day, my cousin, if we had your five whiggishly inclined gentlemen with us we might yet make a fight for it." And he bit his lip and looked doubtfully at the company.

"We will fight nane," said the Deacon. "We are men o' peace, traivelling to further our lawful calling. Are we to dip our hands in bluid to please a Hieland Jaicobite?" The two Campbells groaned in acquiescence, but I thought I saw a glint of something not peaceful in Graham's eye.

"But ye are Scots folk," said Ewan, with a soft, wheedling note in his voice. "Ye will never see a countryman fall into the hands of redcoat English soldiers?"

"It's the law o' the land," said a Campbell, "and what for should we resist it to pleasure you? Besides, we are merchants and no fechtin' tinklers."

I saw Ewan turn his head and look down the road. Far off in the stillness of the grey weather one could hear the sound of feet on the hill gravel.

"Gentlemen," he cried, turning to them with a last appeal, "you see I have no way of escape. You are all proper men, and I beseech you in God's name to help a poor gentleman in his last extremity. If I could win past the gentry in front, there would be the sea coast straight before, where even now there lies a vessel to take me to a kinder country. I cannot think that loyalty to my clan and kin should be counted an offence in the eyes of honest men. I do not know whether you are Highland or Lowland, but you are at least men, and may God do to you as you do to me this day. Who will stand with me?"

I sprang to his side, and the four of us stood looking down the road, where afar off came into sight the moving shapes of the foe.

Then he turned again to the others, crying out a word in Gaelic. I do not know what it was, but it must have gone to their hearts' core, for the little man Macneil with a sob came running toward us, and Graham took one step forward and then stopped.

I whispered their names in Ewan's ear and he smiled. Again he spoke in Gaelic, and this time Graham could forbear no more, but with an answering word in the same tongue he flung himself from his horse and came to our side. The two red-headed Campbells stared in some perplexity, their eyes bright with emotion and their hands twitching towards their belts.

Meantime the sound of men came nearer and the game grew desperate. Again Ewan cried in Gaelic, and this time it was low entreaty, which to my ignorant ears sounded with great pathos. The men looked at the Deacon and at us, and then with scarlet faces they too dropped to the ground and stepped to our backs.

Out of the mist came a line of dark weather-browned faces and the gleam of bright coats. "Will you not come?" Ewan cried to the Deacon.

"I will see no blood shed," said the man, with set lips.

And then there was the sharp word of command, and ere ever I knew, the rattle of shots; and the next moment we were rushing madly down on the enemy.

I have no clear mind of what happened. I know that the first bullet passed through my coat collar and a second grazed my boot. I heard one of the Highlanders cry out and clap his hand to his ear, and then we were at death grips. I used my sword as I could, but I had better have had a dirk, for we were wrestling for dear life, and there was no room for fine play. I saw dimly the steel of Ewan and the Highlanders gleam in the rain; I heard Graham roaring like a bull as he caught at the throat of an opponent. And then all was mist and madness and a great horror. I fell over a little brink of rock with a man a-top of me, and there we struggled till I choked the life out of him. After that I remember nothing till I saw the air clear and the road vacant before us.

Two bodies lay on the heath, besides the one I had accounted for in the hollow. The rest of the soldiers had fled down the pass, and Ewan had his way of escape plain to see. But never have I seen such a change in men. My cousin's coat was red and torn, his shoes all but cut from his feet. A little line of blood trickled over his flushed brow, but he never heeded it, for his eyes burned with the glory of battle. So, too, with his followers, save that one had a hole in his ear and the other a broken arm, which they minded as little as midge bites. But how shall I tell of my companions? The two Campbells sat on the ground nursing wounds, with wild red hair dishevelled and hoarse blasphemy on their lips. Every now and then one would raise his head and cry some fierce word of triumph. Graham had a gash on his cheek, but he was bending his sword point on the ground and calling Ewan his blood brother. The little man Macneil, who had fought like a Trojan, was whimpering with excitement, rubbing his eyes, and staring doubtfully at the heavens. But the Deacon, that man of peace – what shall I say of him? He stood some fifty yards down the pass, peering through the mist at the routed fugitives, his naked sword red in his hand, his whole apparel a ruin of blood and mire, his neatly-dressed hair flying like a beldame's. There he stood hurling the maddest oaths. "Hell!" he cried. "Come back and I'll learn ye, my lads. Wait on, and I'll thraw every neck and give the gleds a feed this day."

Ewan came up and embraced me. "Your Whigamores are the very devil, cousin, and have been the saving of me. But now we are all in the same boat, so we had better improve our time. Come, lads!" he cried, "is it for the seashore and a kinder land?"

And all except the Deacon cried out in Gaelic the word of consent, which, being interpreted, is "Lead, and we follow."

THE BLACK FISHERS

Once upon a time, as the story goes, there lived a man in Gledsmuir, called Simon Hay, who had born to him two sons. They were all very proper men, tall, black-avised, formed after the right model of stalwart folk, and by the account of the place in fear of neither God nor devil. He himself had tried many trades before he found the one which suited his talent; but in the various professions of herd, gamekeeper, drover, butcher, and carrier he had not met with the success he deserved. Some makeshift for a conscience is demanded sooner or later in all, and this Simon could not supply. So he flitted from one to the other with decent haste, till his sons came to manhood and settled the matter for themselves. Henceforth all three lived by their wits in defiance of the law, snaring game, poaching salmon, and working evil over the green earth. Hard drinkers and quick fighters, all men knew them and loved them not. But with it all they kept up a tincture of reputability, foreseeing their best interest. Ostensibly their trade was the modest one of the small crofter, and their occasional attendance at the kirk kept within bounds the verdict of an incensorious parish.

It chanced that in spring, when the streams come down steely blue and lipping over their brims, there came the most halcyon weather that ever man heard of. The air was mild as June, the nights soft and clear, and winter fled hotfoot in dismay. Then these three girded themselves and went to the salmon poaching in the long shining pools of the Callowa in the haughlands below the Dun Craigs. The place was far enough and yet not too far from the town, so that an active walker could go there, have four hours' fishing, and return, all well within the confines of the dark.

On this night their sport was good, and soon the sacks were filled with glittering backs. Then, being drowsy from many nights out o' bed, they bethought them of returning. It would be well to get some hours of sleep before the morning, for they must be up betimes to dispose of their fish. The hardship of such pursuits lies not in the toil but the fate which hardens expediency into necessity.

At the strath which leads from the Callowa vale to Gled they halted. By crossing the ridge of hill they would save three good miles and find a less frequented path. The argument was irresistible; without delay they left the highway and struck over the bent and heather. The road was rough, but they were near its end, and a serene glow of conscious labour began to steal over their minds.

Near the summit is a drystone dyke which girdles the breast of the hill. It was a hard task to cross with a great load of fish even for the young men. The father, a man of corpulent humours and maturing years, was nigh choked with his burden. He mounted slowly and painfully on the loose stones, and prepared to jump. But his foothold was insecure, and a stone slipped from its place. Then something terrible followed. The sack swung round from his neck, and brought him headlong to the ground. When the sons ran forward he was dead as a herring, with a broken neck.

The two men stood staring at one another in hopeless bewilderment. Here was something new in their experience, a disturbing element in their plans. They had just the atom of affection for their fellow worker to make them feel the practical loss acutely. If they went for help to the nearest town, time would be lost and the salmon wasted; and indeed it was not unlikely that some grave suspicion would attach to their honourable selves.

They held a hurried debate. At first they took refuge in mutual recriminations and well-worn regrets. They felt that some such sentiments were due to the modicum of respectability in their reputations. But their minds were too practical to linger long in such barren ground. It was demanded by common feeling of decency that they should have their father's body taken home. But were there any grounds for such feeling? None. It could not matter much to their father, who was the only one really concerned, whether he was removed early or late. On the other hand, they had trysted to meet a man seven miles down the water at five in the morning. Should he be disappointed? Money was money; it was a hard world, where one had to work for beer and skittles; death was a misfortune, but not exactly a deterrent. So picking up the old man's sack, they set out on their errand.

It chanced that the shepherd of the Lowe Moss returned late that night from a neighbour's house, and in crossing the march dyke came on the body. He was much shocked, for he recognised it well as the mortal remains of one who had once been a friend. The shepherd was a dull man and had been drinking; so as the subject was beyond his special domain he dismissed its consideration till some more convenient season. He did not trouble to inquire into causes – there were better heads than his for the work – but set out with all speed for the town.

The procurator fiscal had been sitting up late reading in the works of M. de Maupassant, when he was aroused by a constable, who told him that a shepherd had come from the Callowa with news that a man lay dead at the back of a dyke. The procurator fiscal rose with much grumbling, and wrapped himself up for the night errand. Really, he reflected with Hedda Gabler, people should not do these things nowadays. But, once without, his feelings changed. The clear high space of the sky and the whistling airs of night were strange and beautiful to a town-bred man. The round hills and grey whispering river touched his poetic soul. He began to feel some pride in his vocation.

When he came to the spot he was just in the mood for high sentiment. The sight gave him a shudder. The full-blown face ashen with the grip of death jarred on his finer sensibilities. He remembered to have read of just such a thing in the works of M. Guy. He felt a spice of anger at fate and her cruel ways.

"How sad!" he said; "this old man, still hale and fit to enjoy life, goes out into the hills to visit a friend. On returning he falls in with those accursed dykes of yours; there is a slip in the darkness, a cry, and then – he can taste of life no more. Ah, Fate, to men how bitter a taskmistress," he quoted with a far-off classical reminiscence.

The constable said nothing. He knew Simon Hay well, and guessed shrewdly how he had come by his death, but he kept his own counsel. He did not like to disturb fine sentiment, being a philosopher in a small way.

The two fishers met their man and did their business all in the most pleasant fashion. On their way they had discussed their father's demise. It would interfere little with their profits, for of late he had grown less strong and more exacting. Also, since death must come to all, it was better that it should have taken their father unawares. Otherwise he might have seen fit to make trouble about the cottage which was his, and which he had talked of leaving elsewhere. On the whole, the night's events were good; it only remained to account for them.

It was with some considerable trepidation that they returned to the town in the soft spring dawning. As they entered, one or two people looked out and pointed to them, and nodded significantly to one another. The two men grew hotly uncomfortable. Could it be possible? No. All must have happened as they expected. Even now they would be bringing their father home. His finding would prove the manner of his death. Their only task was to give some reason for its possibility.

At the bridge end a man came out and stood before them.

"Stop," he cried. "Tarn and Andra Hay, prepare to hear bad news. Your auld faither was fund this morning on the back o' Callowa hill wi' a broken neck. It's a sair affliction. Try and thole it like men."

The two grew pale and faltering. "My auld faither," said the chorus. "Oh ye dinna mean it. Say it's no true. I canna believe it, and him aye sae guid to us. What'll we dae wi'oot him?"

"Bear up, my poor fellows," and the minister laid a hand on the shoulder of one. "The Lord gave and the Lord has taken away." He had a talent for inappropriate quotation.

But for the two there was no comfort. With dazed eyes and drawn faces, they asked every detail, fervently, feverishly. Then with faltering voices they told of how their father had gone the night before to the Harehope shepherd's, who was his cousin, and proposed returning in the morn. They bemoaned their remissness, they bewailed his kindness; and then, attended by condoling friends, these stricken men went down the street, accepting sympathy in every public.

SUMMER WEATHER

In a certain year the prices of sheep at Gledsmuir sank so low that the hearts of the farmers were troubled; and one – he of Clachlands – sought at once to retrieve his fortunes and accepted an understudy. This was the son of a neighbouring laird, a certain John Anthony Dean, who by way of preparing himself for the possession of a great moorland estate thought it well to learn something of the life of the place. He was an amiable and idyllic young man, whom I once had the pleasure of knowing well. His interest was centred upon the composition of elegant verses, and all that savoured of the poetic was endeared to his soul. Therefore he had long admired the shepherd's life from afar; the word "pastoral" conjured up a fragrant old-time world; so in a mood pleasantly sentimental he embarked upon the unknown. I need not describe his attainments as sheep farmer or shepherd; he scarcely learned the barest rudiments; and the sage master of Clachlands trusted him only when he wrought under his own vigilant eye. Most of his friends had already labelled him a good-natured fool, and on the whole I do not feel ready to dispute the verdict. But that on one occasion he was not a fool, that once at least Mr John Anthony Dean rose out of his little world into the air of the heroic, this tale is written to show.

It was a warm afternoon in late June, and, his dog running at heel, he went leisurely forth to the long brown ridges of moor. The whole valley lay sweltering in torrid heat; even there, on the crest of a ridge, there was little coolness. The hills shimmered blue and indeterminate through the haze, and the waters of a little loch not a mile away seemed part of the colourless benty upland. He was dressed in light flannels and reasonable shoes – vastly unlike the professional homespuns and hobnailed boots; but even he felt the airless drought and the flinty, dusty earth underfoot, and moderated his pace accordingly.

He was in a highly cheerful frame of mind, and tranquil enjoyment shone in his guileless face. On this afternoon certain cousins were walking over from his father's lodge to visit him at his labours. He contemplated gaily the prospect of showing them this upland Arcady, himself its high priest and guardian. Of all times afternoon was the season when its charm was most dominant, when the mellow light lay on the far lines of mountain, and the streams were golden and russet in the pools. Then was the hour when ancient peace filled all the land, and the bleat of sheep and the calling of birds were but parts of a primeval silence. Even this dried-up noonday moor had the charm of an elder poetry. The hot smell of earth, the glare of the sun from the rocks, were all incidents in pastoral. Even thus, he mused, must the shepherds of Theocritus have lived in that land of downs where the sunburnt cicala hummed under the brown grass.

Some two miles from home he came to the edge of a shallow dale in whose midst a line of baked pebbles and tepid pools broke the monotonous grey. The heat was overpowering, and a vague longing for cool woods and waters stole into his mind. But the thought that this would but add to the tan of his complexion gave him comfort. He pictured the scene of his meeting with his friends; how he would confront them as the bronzed and seasoned uplander with an indescribable glamour of the poetic in his air. He was the man who lived with nature amid the endless moors, who carried always with him the romance of the inexplicable and the remote.

Such pleasing thoughts were roughly broken in on by the sight of his dog. It was a finely bred sheep-collie, a prize-taker, and not the least costly part of his equipment. Already once in that burning summer the animal had gone into convulsions and come out of them weak and foolish. Now it lay stiffened in exactly the same way, its tongue lolling feebly, and flecks of white on its parched jaw. His sensibilities were affected, and he turned from the pitiable sight.

When he looked again it was creeping after him with tail between legs and its coat damp with sweat. Then at the crossing of a gate he missed the sound of it and looked back. There it lay again, this time more rigid than before, apparently not far from the extremities of death. His face grew grave, for he had come to like the creature and he would regret its loss.

But even as he looked the scene changed utterly. The stiffness relaxed, and before he knew the dog was on its feet and coming towards him. He rubbed his eyes with sheer amazement; for the thing looked like an incarnate devil. Its eyes glowered like coals, and its red cavern of a mouth was lined with a sickening froth. Twice its teeth met with a horrid snap as it rushed straight for him at an incredible swiftness. His mind was all but numbed, but some instinct warned him against suffering the beast to cut him off from home. The far dyke was the nearer, but he chose to make rather for the one he had already crossed. By a hairbreadth he managed to elude the rush and let the thing pass – then with a very white face and a beating heart he ran for his life.

By a kind chance the thing had run many yards ere it saw his flight. Then it turned and with great leaps like a greyhound made after him. He heard it turn, heard every bound, with the distinctness of uttermost fear. His terror was lest it should gain on him unknown, and overpower him before he had chance to strike. Now he was almost at the dyke; he glanced round, saw the thing not five yards from him, and waited. The great scarlet jaws seemed to rise in the air before him, and with all his power he brought his thick crook down full athwart them. There was something dead and unearthly about these mad jaws; he seemed to be striking lifeless yet murderous flesh, and even as his stick crashed on the teeth his heart was sick with loathing. But he had won his end; for a second the brute fell back, and he leaped on the dyke.

It was a place built of loose moor stones, and on one larger than the rest he took his stand. He dare not trust a further chase; here he must weary the thing out, or miserably perish. Meantime it was rising again, its eyes two blazing pools of fire. Two yards forward it dragged itself, then sprang clear at his throat. He struck with all his might, but the blow missed its forehead, and, hitting the gums, sufficed only to turn it slightly aside, so that it fell on the wall two feet on his left. He lashed at it with frenzied strength, till groaning miserably it rolled off and lay panting on the turf.

The sun blazed straight on his bare head (for he had lost his cap in the chase), and sweat blinded his eyes. He felt ill, giddy, and hopelessly sick of heart. He had seen nothing of madness before in man or animal; the thing was an awful mystery, a voiceless, incredible horror. What not two hours before had been a friendly, sensible collie now lay blinking at him with devouring eyes and jaws where foam was beginning to be dyed with blood. He calculated mechanically on each jump, and as the beast neared him his stick fell with stiff, nerveless force. To tell the truth, the man was numb with terror; his impulse was to sink to the ground; had death faced him in any form less repulsive than this assuredly he would not have striven against it.

It is a weak figure of speech to say that to him each minute seemed of an hour's length. He had no clear sense of time at all. His one sensation was an overmastering horror which directed his aim almost without his knowledge. Three times the thing leaped on him; three times he struck, and it slipped with claws grating on the stone. Then it turned and raced round a circle of heather, with its head between its forepaws like a runaway horse. The man dropped on his knees to rest, looking intently at the circling speck, now far away, now not a dozen yards distant. He vainly hoped that it would tire or leave him; vainly, for of a sudden it made for the wall and he had barely time to get to his feet before it was upon him. This time he struck it down without difficulty, for it was somewhat exhausted; but he noted with new terror that instead of leaping and falling back with open jaws, its teeth had shut with a snap as it neared him. Henceforth he must ward more closely, or the teeth might graze his flesh.

But his strength was failing, and the accursed brute seemed to grow more active and incessant. His knees ached with the attitude, and his arm still trembled with utter fear. From what he told me himself, and from the known hours of his starting and returning, he must have remained not less than two hours perched on that scorching dyke. It is probable that the heat made him somewhat light-headed and that his feet shuffled on the granite. At any rate as the thing came on him with new force he felt the whole fabric crumble beneath him, and the next second was sprawling on his back amid a ruin of stones.

He was aware of a black body hurling on the top of him as he struck feebly in the air. For a moment of agony he waited to be torn, feeling himself beyond resistance. But no savage teeth touched him, and slowly and painfully he raised his head. To his amazement he saw the dog tearing across the moorland in the direction of home.

He was conscious at once of relief, safety, a sort of weak, hysterical joy. Then his delight ceased abruptly, and he scrambled to his feet with all haste. The thing was clearly running for the farm-town, and there in the stack-yard labourers were busied with building hayricks – the result of a premature summer. In the yard women would be going to and fro, and some of the Clachlands children playing. What if the mad brute should find its way thither! There could be no issue but the most dismal tragedy.

Now Mr John Anthony Dean was, speaking generally, a fool, but for one short afternoon he proved himself something more. For he turned and ran at his utmost speed after the fleeing dog. His legs were cramped and tottering, he was weak with fear, and his head was giddy with the sun; but he strained every muscle as if he ran for his own life and not for the life of others. His wind was poor at the best, and soon he was panting miserably, with a parched throat and aching chest; but with set teeth he kept up the chase, seeing only a black dot vanishing across the green moorland.

By some strange freak of madness the brute stopped for a second, looked round and waited. Its pursuer was all but helpless, labouring many yards behind; and had it attacked, it could have met little resistance. The man's heart leaped to his mouth, but – and to his glory I tell it – he never slackened pace. The thing suffered him to approach it, he had already conjured up the awful prospect of that final struggle, when by another freak it turned and set off once more for home.

To me it seems a miracle that under that blazing sun he ever reached the farm; but the fact remains, that when the dog three minutes later dashed into an empty yard, the man followed some seconds behind it. By the grace of God the place was void; only a stray hen cackled in the summer stillness. Without swerving an inch it ran for the stable and entered the open door. With a last effort the man came up on its heels, shut the bolt, and left it secure.

He scarcely felt that his toil was ended, so painful was his bodily exhaustion. He had never been a strong man in the common sense, and now his heart seemed bursting, his temples throbbed with pain, and all the earth seemed to dance topsy-turvy. But an unknown hardiness of will seemed to drive him on to see this tragic business to an end. It was his part to shoot the dog there and then, to put himself out of anxiety and the world out of danger. So he staggered to the house, found it deserted – one and all being busy in the stack-yard – took down the gun from above the mantelpiece, and, slipping a cartridge in each barrel, hurried out with shambling legs.

He looked in through the stable window, but no dog was there. Cautiously he opened the door, and peered into the blackness of the stalls, but he could see nothing; then, lifting his eyes by chance to the other window, he saw a sash in fragments and the marks of a sudden leap. With a wild horror he realized that the dog was gone.

He rushed to the hill road, but the place was vacant of life. Then with a desperate surmise he ran to the path which led to the highway. At first he saw nothing, so unsettled was his vision; then something grew upon his sight – a black object moving swiftly amid the white dust.

There was but one course for him. He summoned his strength for a hopeless effort, and set off down the long dazzling roadway in mad pursuit. By this path his cousins were coming; even now the brute might be on them, and in one moment of horror he saw the lady to whom he was devoted the prey of this nameless thing of dread. At this point he lost all control of his nerves; tears of weakness and terror ran over his face; but still he ran as fast as his failing strength suffered – faster, for an overmastering fear put a false speed into his limbs and a deceptive ease in his breast. He cried aloud that the beast might turn on him, for he felt that in any case his duration was but a thing of seconds. But he cried in vain, for the thing heeded him not but vanished into the wood, as he rounded the turn of hill.

Halfway down the descent is a place shaded with thick trees, cool, green, and mossy, a hermitage from the fiercest sun. The grass is like a shorn lawn, and a little stream tinkles in a bed of grey stones. Into this cold dell the man passed from the glare without, and the shock refreshed him. This, as it chanced, was his salvation. He increased his speed, still crying hoarsely the animal's name. When he came once more into the white dust the brute was not fifty yards from him, and as he yelled more desperately, it stopped, turned, saw him, and rushed back to the attack.

He fell on his knees from extreme weakness, and waited with his gun quivering at shoulder. Now it raked the high heavens, now it was pointed to the distant hills. His hand shook like a child's, and in his blindness he crushed the stock almost against his throat. Up the highway meantime came those ravening jaws, nearer and ever nearer. Like a flash the whole picture of the future lay before him – himself torn and dying, the wild thing leaving him and keeping its old course till it met his friends, and then – more horror and death. And all hung on two cartridges and his uncertain aim.

His nervousness made him draw the trigger when the brute was still many yards away. The shot went clear over its head to spend itself in the empty air. In desperation he nuzzled the stock below his chin, holding it tight till he was all but choked, and waited blindly. The thing loomed up before him in proportions almost gigantic; it seemed to leap to and fro, and blot out the summer heavens. He knew he was crazy; he knew, too, that life was in the balance, and that a random aim would mean a short passage to another world. Two glaring eyes shone out of the black mass, the centre, as it were, of its revolutions. With all his strength he drew the point to them and fired. Suddenly the fire seemed to go out, and the twin lights were darkened.

When the party of pretty young women in summer raiment came up the path a minute later, they saw something dark in the mid-road, and on coming nearer found that it was their cousin. But he presented a strange appearance, for in place of the elegant, bronzed young man they knew, they found a broken-down creature with a bleeding throat and a ghastly face, sitting clutching a gun and weeping hysterically beside a hideous, eyeless dog with a shattered jaw which lay dead on the ground.

Such is the tale of Mr John Anthony Dean and his doings on that afternoon of summer. Yet it must be told – and for human nature's sake I regret it – that his sudden flash into the heroic worked no appreciable difference on his ways. He fled the hill country that very month, and during the next winter published a book of very minor poetry (dedicated to his cousin, Miss Phyllis), which contained an execrable rondeau on his adventure, with the refrain – "From Canine Jaws", wherein the author likened the dog to Cerberus, himself to "strong Amphitryon's son", and wound up with grateful thanksgiving to the "Muse" for his rescue. As I said before, it is not my business to apologise for Mr Dean; but it is my privilege to note this proof of the heroic inconsistency of man.

THE OASIS IN THE SNOW

This tale was told to me by the shepherd of Callowa, when I sheltered once in his house against an April snowstorm – for he who would fish Gled in spring must fear neither wind nor weather. The shepherd was a man of great height, with the slow, swinging gait, the bent carriage, the honest eyes, and the weather-tanned face which are the marks of his class. He talked little, for life is too lonely or too serious in these uplands for idle conversation; but when once his tongue was loosened, under the influence of friendship or drink, he could speak as I have heard few men ever talk, for his mind was a storehouse of forty years' experience, the harvest of an eye shrewd and observant. This story he told me as we sat by the fire, and looked forth every now and then drearily on the weather.

They crack about snaw-storms nowadays, and ken nauch about them. Maybe there's a wee pickle driftin' and a road blockit, and there's a great cry about the terrible storm. But, lord, if they had kenned o' the storms I've kenned o' they would speak a wee thing mair serious and respectfu'. And bodies come here i' the simmer and gang daft about the bonny green hills, as they ca' them, and think life here sae quate and peacefu', as if the folk here had nocht to dae but daunder roond their hills and follow their wark as trig and easy as if they were i' the holms o' Clyde and no i' the muirs o' Gled. But they dinna ken, and weel for them, how cauld and hungry and cruel are the hills, how easy a man gangs to his death i' thae braw glens, how the wind stings

93

i' the morn and the frost bites at nicht, o' the bogs and sklidders and dreich hillsides, where there's life neither for man nor beast.

Weel, about this story, it was yince in a Februar' mony year syne that it a' happened, when I was younger and lichter on my feet and mair gleg i' the seein'.

Ye mind Doctor Crichton – he's deid thae ten 'ear, but he was a braw doctor in his time. He could cure when anither was helpless, and the man didna leeve whae wad ride further on less errand.

Now the doctor was terrible keen on fishin' and shootin' and a' manner o' sport. I've heard him say that there were three things he likit weel abune ithers. Yin was the back o' a guid horse, anither a guid water and a clear wast wind, and the third a snawy day and a shot at the white hares. He had been crakin' on me for mony a day to gang wi' him, but I was thrang that 'ear wi' cairtin' up hay for the sheep frae lower doon the glens and couldna dae 't. But this day I had trystit to gang wi' him, for there had been a hard frost a' the week, and the hares on the hills wad be in graund fettle. Ye ken the way o' the thing. Yae man keeps yae side o' the hill and the ither the ither, and the beasts gang atween them, back and forrit. Whiles ye'll see them pop round the back o' a dyke and aff again afore ye can get a shot. It's no easy wark, for the skins o' the craturs are ill to tell frae the snawy grund, and a man taks to hae a gleg ee afore he can pick them oot, and a quick hand ere he can shoot. But the doctor was rale skilfu' at it and verra proud, so we set aff brisk-like wi' our guns.

It was snawin' lichtly when we startit, and ere we had gone far it begood to snaw mair. And the air was terrible keen, and cut like a scythe-blade. We were weel wrappit up and walkit a' our pith, but our fingers were soon like to come off, and it was nane sae easy to handle the gun. We tried the Wildshaw Hichts first, and got nane there, though we beat up and doon, and were near smoored wi' snaw i' the gullies. I didna half like the look o' things, for it wasna canny that there should be nae hares, and, forbye, the air was gettin' like a rusty saw to the face. But the doctor wad hear naething o' turnin' back, for he had plenty o' speerit, had the man, and said if we didna get hares on yae hill we wad get them on the ither.

At that time ye'll mind that I had twae dowgs, baith guid but verra contrar' in natur'. There was yin ca'ed Tweed, a fine, canty sort o' beast, very freendly to the bairns, and gien to followin' me to kirk and things o' that sort. But he was nae guid for the shootin', for he was mortal feared at the sound o' a gun, and wad rin hame as he were shot. The ither I ca'ed Voltaire, because he was terrible against releegion. On Sabbath day about kirk time he gaed aff to the hills, and never lookit near the hoose till I cam back. But he was a guid sheep dowg and, forbye, he was broken till the gun, and verra near as guid's a retriever. He wadna miss a day's shootin' for the warld, and mony a day he's gane wi'oot his meat ower the heid o't. Weel, on this day he had startit wi' us and said nae words about it; but noo he began to fa' ahint, and I saw fine he didna like the business. I kenned the dowg never did onything wi'oot a guid reason, and that he was no easy to fricht, so I began to feel uneasy. I stopped for a meenute to try him, and pretended I was gaun to turn hame. He cam rinnin' up and barkit about my legs as pleased as ye like, and when I turned again he looked awfu' dowie.

I pointed this oot to the doctor, but he paid nae attention. "Tut, tut," says he, "if ye're gaun to heed a dowg's havers, we micht gie a'thing up at yince."

"It's nae havers," I said, hot-like, for I didna like to hear my dowg misca'ed. "There's mair sense in that beast than what's in a heap o' men's heids."

"Weel, weel," he says, "sae let it be. But I'm gaun on, and ye can come or no, just as ye like."

"Doctor," says I again, "ye dinna ken the risk ye're rinnin'. I'm a better juidge o' the wather than you, and I tell ye that I'm feared at this day. Ye see that the air is as cauld's steel, and yet there's mist a' in front o' ye and ahint. Ye ken the auld owercome, 'Rouk is snaw's wraith,' and if we dinna see a fearsome snaw afore this day's dune, I'll own my time's been wastit."

But naething wad move him, and I had to follow him for fair shame. Sune after, too, we startit some hares, and though we didna get ony, it set the excitement o' the sport on us. I sune got as keen as himsel', and sae we trampit on, gettin' farther intil the hills wi' every step, and thinkin' naething about the snaw.

We tried the Gledscleuch and got naething, and syne we gaed on to the Allercleuch, and no anither beast did we see. Then we struck straucht for the Cauldhope Loch, which lies weel hoddit in hills miles frae ony man. But there we cam nae better speed, for a' we saw was the frozen loch and the dowie threshes and snaw, snaw everywhere, lyin' and fa'in'. The day had grown waur, and still that dour man wadna turn back. "Come on," says he, "the drift's clearin', and in a wee we'll be on clear grund;" and he steppit oot as he were on the laigh road. The air wasna half as cauld, but thick just like a nicht in hairst; and though there wasna muckle snaw fa'in' yet, it felt as though there were miles o' 't abune in the cluds and pressin' doun to the yirth. Forbye, it was terrible sair walkin', for though the snaw on the grund wasna deep, it was thick and cloggin'. So on we gaed, the yin o' us in high fettle, the ither no verra carin', till we cam to the herd's shielin' o' the Lanely Bield, whilk lies in the very centre o' the hills, whaur I had never been afore.

We chappit at the door and they took us in. The herd was a dacent man, yin Simon Trumbull, and I had seen him aften at kirk and market. So he bade us welcome, and told us to get our claes dried, for we wadna gang anither step that nicht. Syne his wife made us tea, and it helpit us michtily, for we had drank a' our whisky lang syne. They had a great fire roarin' up the lum, and I was sweired, I can tell ye, to gang oot o' the warm place again into the ill wather.

But I must needs be aff if I was to be hame that nicht, and keep my wife from gaun oot o' her mind. So I gets up and buttons to my coat.

"Losh, man," says the herd, "ye're never thinkin' o' leavin'. It'll be the awfu'est nicht that ever man heard tell o'. I've herdit thae hills this mony 'ear, and I never saw sic tokens o' death i' the air. I've my sheep fauldit lang syne, and my hoose weel stockit, or I wadna bide here wi' an easy hert."

"A' the mair need that I should gang," says I, "me that has naething dune. Ye ken fine my wife. She wad die wi' fricht, if I didna come hame."

Simon went to the door and opened it. It blew back on the wa', and a solid mass o' snaw fell on the floor. "See that," he says. "If ye dinna believe me, believe your ain een. Ye need never think o' seein' Callowa the nicht."

"See it or no," said I, "I'll hae to try 't. Ye'd better bide, doctor; there's nae cause for you to come wi' me."

"I'll gang wi' you," he said. "I brocht ye intil this, and I'll see ye oot o't." And I never liked the man sae weel as at the word.

When the twae o' us walkit frae that hoose it was like walkin' intil a drift o' snaw. The air was sae thick that we couldna richt see the separate flakes. It was just a great solid mass sinkin' ever doun, and as heavy as a thousand ton o' leid. The breath went frae me at the verra outset. Something clappit on my chest, and I had nocht to dae but warstle on wi' nae mair fushion than a kittlin'. I had a grip o' the doctor's hand, and muckle we needit it, for we wad sune hae been separate and never mair heard o'. My dowg Voltaire, whae was gien for ordinar' to rinnin' wide and playin' himsel', kept close rubbin' against my heels. We were miles frae hame, and unless the thing cleared there was sma' chance o' us winnin' there. Yae guid thing, there was little wind, but just a saft, even fa'; so it wasna so bad as though it had been a fierce driftin'. I had a general kind o' glimmer o' the road, though I had never been in thae hills afore. If we held doun by the Lanely Bield Burn we wad come to the tap o' the Stark

Water, whilk cam into Gled no a mile abune Callowa. So on we warstled, prayin' and greetin' like bairns, wi' scarce a thocht o' what we were daein'.

"Whaur are we?" says the doctor in a wee, and his voice sounded as though he had a naipkin roond his mouth.

"I think we should be somewhere near the Stark heid," said I. "We're gaun doun, and there's nae burn hereaways but it."

"But I aye thocht the Stark Glen was a' sklidders at the heid," said he; "and this is as saft a slope as a hoose riggin'."

"I canna help that," says I. "It maun e'en be it, or we've clean missed the airt."

So on we gaed again, and the snaw aye got deeper. It wasna awfu' saft, so we didna sink far as we walkit, but it was terrible wearin'. I sune was sae tired that I could scarce drag mysel'; forbye being frichtit oot o' my senses. But the doctor was still stoot and hopefu', and I just followed him.

Suddenly, ere ever we kenned, the slope ceased, and we were walkin' on flat grund. I could scarce believe my een, but there it was at my feet, as high as a kitchen floor. But the queer thing was that while a' around was deep snaw, this place was a' but bare, and here and there rigs o' green land stuck oot.

"What in the warld's this?" says I, as I steppit oot boldly, and I turned to my companion. When I saw him I was fair astonished. For his face was white as the snaw, and he was tremblin' to his fingers.

"Ye're no feared, are ye?" I asked. "D 'ye no ken guid land when ye see 't?"

His teeth were chattering in his heid. "You hae na sense to be feared. The Almichty help us, but I believe we're daein' what nae man ever did afore."

I never saw sae queer a place. The great wecht o' snaw was still fa'in' on us, but it seemed to disappear when it cam to the grund. And our feet when we steppit aye sank a wee bit, but no in snaw. The feel i' the air wasna cauld, but if onything 't was het and damp. The sweat began to rin doon aff my broo, and I could hear the man ahint me pantin' like a broken-winded horse. I lookit roond me for the dowg, but nae dowg was to be seen; for at the first step we took on the queer land he had ta'en himsel' aff. I didna like the look o't, for it wad hae ta'en muckle to drive the beast frae my side.

Every now and then we cam on a wee hillock whaur the snaw lay deeper, but the spaces atween were black and saft, and crunkled aneath the feet. Ye ken i' the spring about the burn-heids how the water rins oot o' the grund, and a' the colour o' the place is a sodden grey. Weel, 't was the same here. There was a seepin', dreepin' feel i' the grund whilk made it awesome to the eye. Had I been i' my clear senses, I wad hae been rale puzzled about the maitter, but I was donnered wi' the drifts and the weariness, and thocht only o' gettin' by 't. But sune a kind o' terror o' the thing took me. Every time my feet touched the grund, as I walkit, a groo gae'd through my body. I grat wi' the fair hate o' the place, and when I lookit at my neebor it didna mak me better. For there he was gaun along shakin' like a tree-tap, and as white 's a clout. It made it waur that the snaw was sae thick i' the air that we couldna see a foot in front. It was like walkin' blindfold roond the tap o' a linn.

Then a' of a sudden the bare grund stopped, and we were flounderin' among deep drifts up to the middle. And yet it was a relief, and my hert was strengthened. By this time I had clean lost coont o' the road, but we keepit aye to the laigh land, whiles dippin' intil a glen and whiles warslin' up a brae face. I had learned frae mony days in hill mists to keep frae gaun roond about. We focht our way like fair deevils, for the terror o' the place ahint had grippit us like a vice. We ne'er spak a word, but wrocht till our herts were like to burst and our een felt fou o' bluid. It got caulder and caulder, and thicker and ever thicker. Hope had lang syne gane frae us, and fricht had ta'en its place. It was just a maitter o' keepin' up till we fell down, and then…

It wasna lang ere they fund us, for find us they did, by God's grace and the help o' the dowg. For the beast went hame and made sic a steer that my wife roused the nearest neebor and got folk startit oot to seek us. And wad ye believe it, the dowg took them to the verra bit. They fund the doctor last, and he lay in his bed for a month and mair wi' the effects. But for mysel', I was nane the waur. When they took me hame, I was put to bed, and sleepit on for twenty hoor, as if I had been streikit oot. They waukened me every six hoor, and put a spoonfu' o' brandy doon my throat, and when a' was feenished, I rase as weel as ever.

It was about fower months after that I had to gang ower to Annandale wi' sheep, and cam back by the hills. It was a road I had never been afore, and I think it was the wildest that ever man trod. I mind it was a warm, bricht day, verra het and wearisome for the walkin'. Bye and bye I cam to a place I seemed to ken, though I had never been there to my mind, and I thocht hoo I could hae seen it afore. Then I mindit that it was abune the heid o' the Stark, and though the snaw had been in my een when I last saw it, I minded the lie o' the land and the saft slope. I turned verra keen to ken what the place was whaur me and the doctor had had sic a fricht. So I went oot o' my way, and climbed yae hill and gaed doun anither, till I cam to a wee rig, and lookit doun on the verra bit.

I just lookit yince, and then turned awa' wi' my hert i' my mooth.

For there below was a great green bog, oozing and blinking in the sun.

THE HERD OF STANDLAN

"When the wind is nigh and the moon is high
    And the mist on the riverside,
Let such as fare have a very good care
    Of the Folk who come to ride.
For they may meet with the riders fleet
    Who fare from the place of dread;
And hard it is for a mortal man
    To sort at ease with the Dead."
The Ballad of Grey Weather.

When Standlan Burn leaves the mosses and hags which gave it birth, it tumbles over a succession of falls into a deep, precipitous glen, whence in time it issues into a land of level green meadows, and finally finds its rest in the Gled. Just at the opening of the ravine there is a pool shut in by high, dark cliffs, and black even on the most sunshiny day. The rocks are never dry but always black with damp and shadow. There is scarce any vegetation save stunted birks, juniper bushes, and draggled fern; and the hoot of owls and the croak of hooded crows is seldom absent from the spot. It is the famous Black Linn where in winter sheep stray and are never more heard of, and where more than once an unwary shepherd has gone to his account. It is an Inferno on the brink of a Paradise, for not a stone's throw off is the green, lawn-like turf, the hazel thicket, and the broad, clear pools, by the edge of which on that July day the Herd of Standlan and I sat drowsily smoking and talking of fishing and the hills. There he told me

101

this story, which I here set down as I remember it, and as it bears repetition.

"D' ye mind Airthur Morrant?" said the shepherd, suddenly.

I did remember Arthur Mordaunt. Ten years past he and I had been inseparables, despite some half-dozen summers difference in age. We had fished and shot together, and together we had tramped every hill within thirty miles. He had come up from the South to try sheep farming, and as he came of a great family and had no need to earn his bread, he found the profession pleasing. Then irresistible fate had swept me southward to college, and when after two years I came back to the place, his father was dead and he had come into his own. The next I heard of him was that in politics he was regarded as the most promising of the younger men, one of the staunchest and ablest upstays of the Constitution. His name was rapidly rising into prominence, for he seemed to exhibit that rare phenomenon of a man of birth and culture in direct sympathy with the wants of the people.

"You mean Lord Brodakers?" said I.

"Dinna call him by that name," said the shepherd, darkly. "I hae nae thocht o' him now. He's a disgrace to his country, servin' the Deil wi' baith hands. But nine year syne he was a bit innocent callant wi' nae Tory deevilry in his heid. Well, as I was sayin', Airthur Morrant has cause to mind that place till his dying day;" and he pointed his finger to the Black Linn.

I looked up the chasm. The treacherous water, so bright and joyful at our feet, was like ink in the great gorge. The swish and plunge of the cataract came like the regular beating of a clock, and though the weather was dry, streams of moisture seamed the perpendicular walls. It was a place eerie even on that bright summer's day.

"I don't think I ever heard the story," I said casually.

"Maybe no," said the shepherd. "It's no yin I like to tell;" and he puffed sternly at his pipe, while I awaited the continuation.

"Ye see it was like this," he said, after a while. "It was just the beginning o' the back end, and that year we had an awfu' spate

102

o' rain. For near a week it poured hale water, and a' doon by Drumeller and the Mossfennan haughs was yae muckle loch. Then it stopped, and an awfu' heat came on. It dried the grund in nae time, but it hardly touched the burns; and it was rale queer to be pourin' wi' sweat and the grund aneath ye as dry as a potato sack, and a' the time the water neither to haud nor bind. A' the waterside fields were clean stripped o' stooks, and a guid wheen hayricks gaed doon tae Berwick, no to speak o' sheep and nowt beast. But that's anither thing.

"Weel, ye'll mind that Airthur was terrible keen on the fishing. He wad gang oot in a' weather, and he wasna feared for ony mortal or naitural thing. Dod, I've seen him in Gled wi' the water rinnin' ower his shouthers yae cauld March day playin' a saumon. He kenned weel aboot the fishing, for he had traivelled in Norroway and siccan outlandish places, where there's a heap o' big fish. So that day – and it was a Setterday tae and far ower near the Sabbath – he maun gang awa' up Standlan Burn wi' his rod and creel to try his luck.

"I was bidin' at that time, as ye mind, in the wee cot-house at the back o' the faulds. I was alane, for it was three year afore I mairried Jess, and I wasna begun yet to the coortin'. I had been at Gledsmuir that day for some o' the new stuff for killing sheep-mawks, and I wasna very fresh on my legs when I gaed oot after my tea that nicht to hae a look at the hill sheep. I had had a bad year on the hill. First the lambin' time was snaw, snaw ilka day, and I lost mair than I wad like to tell. Syne the grass a' summer was so short wi' the drought that the puir beasts could scarcely get a bite and were as thin as pipe-stapples. And then, to crown a', auld Will Broun, the man that helpit me, turned ill wi' his back, and had to bide at hame. So I had twae man's wark on yae man's shouthers, and was nane so weel pleased.

"As I was saying, I gaed oot that nicht, and after lookin' a' the Dun Rig and the Yellow Mire and the back o' Cramalt Craig, I cam down the burn by the road frae the auld faulds. It was geyan dark, being about seven o'clock o' a September nicht, and I keepit weel back frae that wanchancy hole o' a burn. Weel, I was comin' kind o' quick, thinkin' o' supper and a story book that I was readin' at the time, when just abune that place there, at the foot o' the Linn, I saw a man fishing. I wondered what ony body in his senses could be daein' at that time o' nicht in sic a dangerous place, so I gave him a roar and bade him come back. He turned his face round and I saw in a jiffey that it was Mr Airthur.

" 'O, sir,' I cried, 'what for are ye fishing there? The water's awfu' dangerous, and the rocks are far ower slid.'

" 'Never mind, Scott,' he roars back cheery-like. 'I'll take care o' mysel'.'

"I lookit at him for twa-three meenutes, and then I saw by his rod he had yin on, and a big yin tae. He ran it up and doon the pool, and he had uncommon wark wi' 't, for it was strong and there was little licht. But bye and bye he got it almost tae his feet, and was just about to lift it oot when a maist awfu' thing happened. The tackets o' his boots maun hae slithered on the stane, for the next thing I saw was Mr Airthur in the muckle hungry water.

"I dinna exactly ken what happened after that, till I found myself on the very stone he had slipped off. I maun hae come doon the face o' the rocks, a thing I can scarcely believe when I look at them, and a thing no man ever did afore. At ony rate I ken I fell the last fifteen feet or sae, and lichted on my left airm, for I felt it crack like a rotten branch, and an awfu' sairness ran up it.

"Now, the pool is a whirlpool as ye ken, and if anything fa's in, the water first smashes it against the muckle rock at the foot, then it brings it round below the fall again, and syne at the second time it carries it doon the burn. Weel, that was what happened to Mr Airthur. I heard his heid gang dunt on the stane wi' a sound that made me sick. This must hae dung him clean senseless, and indeed it was a wonder it didna knock his brains oot. At ony rate there was nae mair word o' swimming, and he was swirled round below the fa' just like a corp.

"I kenned fine that nae time was to be lost, for if he once gaed doun the burn he wad be in Gled or ever I could say a word, and nae man wad ever see him mair in life. So doon I got on my hunkers on the stane, and waited for the turnin'. Round he came, whirling in the foam, wi' a lang line o' blood across his brow where the stane had cut him. It was a terrible meenute. My heart fair stood still. I put out my airm, and as he passed I grippit him and wi' an awfu' pu' got him out o' the current into the side.

"But now I found that a waur thing still was on me. My left airm was broken, and my richt sae numbed and weak wi' my fall that, try as I micht, I couldna raise him ony further. I thocht I wad burst a blood vessel i' my face and my muscles fair cracked wi' the strain, but I could make nothing o' 't. There he stuck wi' his heid and shouthers abune the water, pu'd close until the edge of a rock.

"What was I to dae? If I once let him slip he wad be into the stream and lost forever. But I couldna hang on here a' nicht, and as far as I could see there wad be naebody near till the mornin', when Ebie Blackstock passed frae the Head o' the Hope. I roared wi' a' my power; but I got nae answer, naething but the rummle o' the water and the whistling o' some whaups on the hill.

"Then I turned very sick wi' terror and pain and weakness and I kenna what. My broken airm seemed a great lump o' burnin' coal. I maun hae given it some extra wrench when I hauled him out, for it was sae sair now that I thocht I could scarcely thole it. Forbye, pain and a', I could hae gone off to sleep wi' fair weariness. I had heard tell o' men sleepin' on their feet, but I never felt it till then. Man, if I hadna warstled wi' mysel, I wad hae dropped off as deid's a peery.

"Then there was the awfu' strain o' keepin' Mr Airthur up. He was a great big man, twelve stone I'll warrant, and weighing a terrible lot mair wi' his fishing togs and things. If I had had the use o' my ither airm I micht hae taen off his jacket and creel and lichtened the burden, but I could do naething. I scarcely like to tell ye how I was tempted in that hour. Again and again I says to mysel, 'Gidden Scott,' says I, 'what do ye care for this man? He's no a drap's bluid to you, and forbye ye'll never be able to save him. Ye micht as weel let him gang. Ye've dune a' ye could. Ye're a brave man, Gidden Scott, and ye've nae cause to be ashamed o' givin' up the fecht.' But I says to mysel again: 'Gidden Scott, ye're a coward. Wad ye let a man die, when there's a breath in your body? Think shame o' yoursel, man.' So I aye kept haudin' on, although I was very near bye wi' 't. Whenever I lookit at Mr Airthur's face, as white 's death and a' blood, and his een sae stelled-like, I got a kind o' groo and felt awfu' pitiful for the bit laddie. Then I thocht on his faither, the auld Lord, wha was sae built up in him, and I couldna bear to think o' his son droonin' in that   awfu'   hole.   So I set mysel to the wark o' keepin' him up a' nicht, though I had nae hope in the matter. It wasna what ye ca' bravery that made me dae 't, for I had nae ither choice. It was just a kind o' dourness that runs in my folk, and a kind o' vexedness for sae young a callant in sic an ill place.

"The nicht was hot and there was scarcely a sound o' wind. I felt the sweat standin' on my face like frost on tatties, and abune me the sky was a' misty and nae mune visible. I thocht very likely that it micht come a thunder shower and I kind o' lookit forrit tae 't. For I was aye feared at lichtning, and if it came that nicht I was bound to get clean dazed and likely tummle in. I was a lonely man wi' nae kin to speak o', so it wouldna maitter muckle.

"But now I come to tell ye about the queer side o' that nicht's wark, whilk I never telled to nane but yoursel, though a' the folk about here ken the rest. I maun hae been geyan weak, for I got into a kind o' doze, no sleepin', ye understand, but awfu' like it. And then a' sort o' daft things began to dance afore my een.

Witches and bogles and brownies and things oot o' the Bible,
and leviathans and brazen bulls – a' cam fleerin' and flauntin' on
the tap o' the water straucht afore me. I didna pay muckle heed
to them, for I half kenned it was a' nonsense, and syne they gaed
awa'. Then an auld wife wi' a mutch and a hale procession o'
auld wives passed, and just about the last I saw yin I thocht I
kenned.

" 'Is that you, grannie?' says I.

" 'Ay, it's me; Gidden,' says she; and as shüre as I'm a leevin'
man, it was my auld grannie, whae had been deid thae sax year.
She had on the same mutch as she aye wore, and the same auld
black stickle in her hand, and, Dod, she had the same snuffbox I
made for her out o' a sheep's horn when I first took to the
herdin'. I thocht she was lookin' rale weel.

" 'Losh, Grannie,' says I, 'where in the warld hae ye come
frae? It's no canny to see ye danderin' about there.'

" 'Ye've been badly brocht up,' she says, 'and ye ken nocht
about it. Is 't no a decent and comely thing that I should get a
breath o' air yince in the while?'

" 'Deed,' said I, 'I had forgotten. Ye were sae like yoursel I
never had a mind ye were deid. And how d' ye like the Guid
Place?'

" 'Wheesht, Gidden,' says she, very solemn-like, 'I'm no
there.'

"Now at this I was fair flabbergasted. Grannie had aye been a
guid contentit auld wumman, and to think that they hadna let
her intil Heeven made me think ill o' my ain chances.

" 'Help us, ye dinna mean to tell me ye're in Hell?' I cries.

" 'No exactly,' says she, 'but I'll trouble ye, Gidden, to speak
mair respectful about holy things. That's a name ye uttered the
noo whilk we dinna daur to mention.'

" 'I'm sorry, Grannie,' says I, 'but ye maun allow it's an
astonishin' thing for me to hear. We aye counted ye shüre, and
ye died wi' the Buik in your hands.'

" 'Weel,' she says, 'it was like this. When I gaed up till the gate o' Heeven a man wi' a lang white robe comes and says, "Wha may ye be?" Says I, "I'm Elspeth Scott." He gangs awa' and consults a wee and then he says, "I think, Elspeth my wumman, ye'll hae to gang doon the brae a bit. Ye're no quite guid eneuch for this place, but ye'll get a very comfortable doonsittin' whaur I tell ye." So off I gaed and cam' to a place whaur the air was like the inside of the glasshouses at the Lodge. They took me in wi'oot a word and I've been rale comfortable. Ye see they keep the bad part o' the Ill Place for the reg'lar bad folk, but they've a very nice halfway house where the likes o' me stop.'

" 'And what kind o' company hae ye?'

" 'No very select,' says she. 'There's maist o' the ministers o' the countryside and a pickle fairmers, tho' the maist o' them are further ben. But there's my son Jock, your ain faither, Gidden, and a heap o' folk from the village, and oh, I'm nane sae bad.'

" 'Is there naething mair ye wad like then, Grannie?'

" 'Oh aye,' says she, 'we've each yae thing which we canna get. It's a' the punishment we hae. Mine's butter. I canna get fresh butter for my bread, for ye see it winna keep, it just melts. So I've to tak jeely to ilka slice, whilk is rale sair on the teeth. Ye'll no hae ony wi' ye?'

" 'No,' I says, 'I've naething but some tobaccy. D' ye want it? Ye were aye fond o' 't.'

" 'Na, na,' says she. 'I get plenty o' tobaccy doon bye. The pipe's never out o' the folks' mouth there. But I'm no speakin' about yoursel, Gidden. Ye're in a geyan ticht place.'

" 'I'm a' that,' I said. 'Can ye no help me?'

" 'I micht try.' And she raxes out her hand to grip mine. I put out mine to tak it, never thinkin' that that wasna the richt side, and that if Grannie grippit it she wad pu' the broken airm and haul me into the water. Something touched my fingers like a hot poker; I gave a great yell; and ere ever I kenned I was awake, a' but off the rock, wi' my left airm aching like hellfire. Mr Airthur

I had let slunge ower the heid and my ain legs were in the water.

"I gae an awfu' whammle and edged my way back though it was near bye my strength. And now anither thing happened. For the cauld water roused Mr Airthur frae his dwam. His een opened and he gave a wild look around him. ' Where am I?' he cries, 'O God!' and he gaed off intil anither faint.

"I can tell ye, sir, I never felt anything in this warld and I hope never to feel anything in anither sae bad as the next meenutes on that rock. I was fair sick wi' pain and weariness and a kind o' fever. The lip-lap o' the water, curling round Mr Airthur, and the great *crush* o' the Black Linn itsel dang me fair silly. Then there was my airm, which was bad eneuch, and abune a' I was gotten into sic a state that I was fleyed at ilka shadow just like a bairn. I felt fine I was gaun daft, and if the thing had lasted anither score o' meenutes I wad be in a madhouse this day. But soon I felt the sleepiness comin' back, and I was off again dozin' and dreamin'.

"This time it was nae auld wumman but a muckle black-avised man that was standin' in the water glowrin' at me. I kenned him fine by the bandy legs o' him and the broken nose (whilk I did mysel), for Dan Kyle the poacher deid thae twae year. He was a man, as I remembered him weel, wi' a great black beard and een that were stuck sae far in his heid that they looked like twae wull-cats keekin' oot o' a hole. He stands and just stares at me, and never speaks a word.

" 'What d' ye want?' I yells, for by this time I had lost a' grip o' mysel. 'Speak, man, and dinna stand there like a dummy.'

" 'I want naething,' he says in a mournfu' sing-song voice; 'I'm just thinkin'.'

" 'Whaur d' ye come frae?' I asked, 'and are ye keepin' weel?'

" 'Weel,' he says bitterly. 'In this warld I was ill to my wife, and twa-three times I near killed a man, and I stole like a pyet, and I was never sober. How d' ye think I should be weel in the next?'

"I was sorry for the man. 'D' ye ken I'm vexed for ye, Dan,' says I; 'I never likit ye whea ye when here, but I'm wae to think ye're sae ill off yonder.'

" 'I'm no alane,' he says. 'There's Mistress Courhope o' the Big House, she's waur. Ye mind she was awfu' fond o' gum-flowers. Weel, she canna keep them Yonder, for they a' melt wi' the heat. She's in an ill way about it, puir body.' Then he broke off. 'Whae's that ye've got there? Is 't Airthur Morrant?'

" 'Ay, it's Airthur Morrant,' I said.

" 'His family's weel kent doon bye,' says he. 'We've maist o' his forbears, and we're expectin' the auld Lord every day. May be we'll sune get the lad himsel.'

" 'That's a damned lee,' says I, for I was angry at the man's presumption.

"Dan lookit at me sorrowfu'-like. 'We'll be gettin' you tae, if ye swear that gate,' says he, 'and then ye'll ken what it's like.'

"Of a sudden I fell into a great fear. 'Dinna say that, Dan,' I cried; 'I'm better than ye think. I'm a deacon, and 'll maybe sune be an elder, and I never swear except at my dowg.'

" 'Tak care, Gidden,' said the face afore me. 'Where I am, a' things are taken into account.'

" 'Then they'll hae a gey big account for you,' says I. 'What-like do they treat you, may be?'

"The man groaned.

" 'I'll tell ye what they dae to ye doon there,' he said. 'They put ye intil a place a' paved wi' stanes and wi' four square walls around. And there's naething in 't, nae grass, nae shadow. And abune you there's a sky like brass. And sune ye get terrible hot and thirsty, and your tongue sticks to your mouth, and your eyes get blind wi' lookin' on the white stane. Then ye gang clean fey, and dad your heid on the ground and the walls to try and kill yoursel. But though ye dae 't till a' eternity ye couldna feel pain. A' that ye feel is just the awfu' devourin' thirst, and the heat and the weariness. And if ye lie doon the ground burns ye and ye're fain to get up. And ye canna lean on the walls for the heat, and bye and bye when ye're fair perished wi' the thing, they tak ye out to try some ither ploy.'

" 'Nae mair,' I cried, 'nae mair, Dan!'

"But he went on malicious-like –

" 'Na, na, Gidden, I'm no dune yet. Syne they tak you to a fine room but awfu' warm. And there's a big fire in the grate and thick woollen rugs on the floor. And in the corner there's a braw feather bed. And they lay ye down on 't, and then they pile on the tap o' ye mattresses and blankets and sacks and great rolls o' woollen stuff miles wide. And then ye see what they're after, tryin' to suffocate ye as they dae to folk that a mad dowg has bitten. And ye try to kick them off, but they're ower heavy, and ye canna move your feet nor your airms nor gee your heid. Then ye gang clean gyte and skirl to yoursel, but your voice is choked and naebody is near. And the warst o' 't is that ye canna die and get it ower. It's like death a hundred times and yet ye're aye leevin'. Bye and bye when they think ye've got eneuch they tak you out and put ye somewhere else.'

" 'Oh,' I cries, 'stop, man, or you'll ding me silly.'

"But he says never a word, just glowrin' at me.

" 'Aye, Gidden, and waur than that. For they put ye in a great loch wi' big waves just like the sea at the Pier o' Leith. And there's nae chance o' soomin', for as sune as ye put out your airms a billow gulfs ye down. Then ye swallow water and your heid dozes round and ye're chokin'. But ye canna die, ye must just thole. And down ye gang, down, down, in the cruel deep, till your heid's like to burst and your een are fu' o' bluid. And there's a' kind o' fearfu' monsters about, muckle slimy things wi' blind een and white scales, that claw at ye wi' claws just like the paws o' a drooned dog. And ye canna get away though ye fecht and fleech, and bye and bye ye're fair mad wi' horror and choking and the feel o' thae awfu' things. Then –'

"But now I think something snapped in my heid, and I went daft in doonricht earnest. The man before me danced about like a lantern's shine on a windy nicht and then disappeared. And I woke yelling like a pig at a killing, fair wud wi' terror, and my skellochs made the rocks ring. I found mysel in the pool a' but yae airm – the broken yin – which had hankit in a crack o' rock. Nae wonder I had been dreaming o' deep waters among the torments o' the Ill Place, when I was in them mysel. The pain in my airm was sae fearsome and my heid was gaun round sae wi' horror that I just skirled on and on, shrieking and groaning wi'oot a thocht what I was daein'. I was as near death as ever I will be, and as for Mr Airthur he was on the very nick o' 't, for by this time he was a' in the water, though I still kept a grip o' him.

"When I think ower it often I wonder how it was possible that I could be here the day. But the Lord's very gracious, and he works in a queer way. For it so happened that Ebie Blackstock, whae had left Gledsmuir an hour afore me and whom I thocht by this time to be snorin' in his bed at the Head o' the Hope, had gone intil the herd's house at the Waterfit, and had got sae muckle drink there that he was sweered to start for hame till aboot half past twal i' the night. Weel, he was comin' up the burnside, gae happy and contentit, for he had nae wife at hame to speir about his on-gaeings, when, as he's telled me himsel, he heard sic an uproar doon by the Black Linn that made him turn pale and think that the Deil, whom he had long served, had gotten him at last. But he was a brave man, was Ebie, and he thinks to himsel that some fellow creature micht be perishin'. So he gangs forrit wi' a' his pith, trying to think on the Lord's Prayer and last Sabbath's sermon. And, lookin' ower the edge, he saw naething for a while, naething but the black water wi' the awfu' yells coming out o' 't. Then he made out something like a heid near the side. So he rins doon by the road, no ower the rocks as I had come, but round by the burnside road, and soon he gets to the pool, where the crying was getting aye fainter and fainter. And then he saw me. And he grips me by the collar, for he was a sensible man, was Ebie, and hauls me oot. If he hadna been geyan strong he couldna hae dune it, for I was a deid wecht, forbye having a heavy man hanging on to me. When he got me up, what was his astonishment to find anither man at the end o' my airm, a man like a corp a' bloody about the heid. So he got us baith out, and we wae baith senseless; and he laid us in a safe bit back frae the water, and syne gaed off for help. So bye and bye we were baith got hame, me to my house and Mr Airthur up to the Lodge."

"And was that the end of it?" I asked.

"Na," said the shepherd. "I lay for twae month there raving wi' brain fever, and when I cam to my senses I was as weak as a bairn. It was many months ere I was mysel again, and my left airm to this day is stiff and no muckle to lippen to. But Mr Airthur was far waur, for the dad he had gotten on the rock was thocht to have broken his skull, and he lay long atween life and death. And the warst thing was that his faither was sae vexed about him that he never got ower the shock, but dee'd afore Airthur was out o' bed. And so when he cam out again he was My Lord, and a monstrously rich man."

The shepherd puffed meditatively at his pipe for a few minutes.

"But that's no a' yet. For Mr Airthur wad tak nae refusal but that I maun gang awa' doon wi' him to his braw house in England and be a land o' factor or steward or something like that. And I had a rale fine cottage a' to mysel, wi' a very bonny gairden and guid wages, so I stayed there maybe sax month and then I gaed up till him. 'I canna bide nae longer,' says I. 'I canna stand this place. It's far ower laigh, and I'm fair sick to get hills to rest my een on. I'm awfu' gratefu' to ye for your kindness, but I maun gie up my job.' He was very sorry to lose me, and was for giein' me a present o' money or stockin' a fairm for me, because he said that it was to me he owed his life. But I wad hae nane o' his gifts. 'It wad be a terrible thing,' I says, ' to tak siller for daein' what ony body wad hae dune out o' pity.' So I cam awa' back to Standlan, and I maun say I'm rale contentit here. Mr Airthur used whiles to write to me and ca' in and see me when he cam North for the shooting; but since he's gane sae far wrang wi' the Tories, I've had naething mair to dae wi' him."

I made no answer, being busy pondering in my mind on the depth of the shepherd's political principles, before which the ties of friendship were as nothing.

"Ay," said he, standing up, "I did what I thocht my duty at the time and I was rale glad I saved the callant's life. But now, when I think on a' the ill he's daein' to the country and the Guid Cause, I whiles think I wad hae been daein' better if I had just drappit him in.

"But whae kens? It's a queer warld." And the shepherd knocked the ashes out of his pipe.

STREAMS OF WATER
IN THE SOUTH

"Like streams of water in the South
Our bondage, Lord, recall."

This is all a tale of an older world and a forgotten countryside. At this moment of time change has come; a screaming line of steel runs through the heather of Noman'sland, and the holiday-maker claims the valleys for his own. But this busyness is but of yesterday, and not ten years ago the fields lay quiet to the gaze of placid beasts and the wandering stars. This story I have culled from the grave of an old fashion, and set it down for the love of a great soul and the poetry of life.

It was at the ford of the Clachlands Water in a tempestuous August, that I, an idle boy, first learned the hardships of the Lammas droving. The shepherd of the Redswirehead, my very good friend, and his three shaggy dogs, were working for their lives in an angry water. The path behind was thronged with scores of sheep bound for the Gledsmuir market, and beyond it was possible to discern through the mist the few dripping dozen which had made the passage. Between raged yards of brown foam coming down from murky hills, and the air echoed with the yelp of dogs and the perplexed cursing of men.

Before I knew I was helping in the task, with water lipping round my waist and my arms filled with a terrified sheep. It was no light task, for though the water was no more than three feet deep it was swift and strong, and a kicking hogg is a sore burden. But this was the only road; the stream might rise higher at any moment; and somehow or other those bleating flocks had to be transferred to their fellows beyond. There were six men at the labour, six men and myself, and all were cross and wearied and heavy with water.

I made my passages side by side with my friend the shepherd, and thereby felt much elated. This was a man who had dwelt all his days in the wilds and was familiar with torrents as with his own doorstep. Now and then a swimming dog would bark feebly as he was washed against us, and flatter his fool's heart that he was aiding the work. And so we wrought on, till by midday I was deadbeat, and could scarce stagger through the surf, while all the men had the same gasping faces. I saw the shepherd look with longing eye up the long green valley, and mutter disconsolately in his beard.

"Is the water rising?" I asked.

"It's no rising," said he, "but I likena the look o' that big, black clud upon Cairncraw. I doubt there's been a shoor up the muirs, and a shoor there means twae mair feet o' water in the Clachlands. God help Sandy Jamieson's lambs, if there is."

"How many are left?" I asked.

"Three, fower – no abune a score and a half," said he, running his eye over the lessened flocks. "I maun try to tak twae at a time."

So for ten minutes he struggled with a double burden, and panted painfully at each return. Then with a sudden swift look upstream he broke off and stood up. "Get ower the water, every yin o' ye, and leave the sheep," he said, and to my wonder every man of the five obeyed his word, for he was known for a wise counsellor in distress.

And then I saw the reason of his command, for with a sudden swift leap forward the Clachlands rose, and flooded up to where I had stood an instant before high and dry.

"It's come," said the shepherd, in a tone of fate, "and there's fifteen no ower yet, and Lord knows how they'll dae 't. They'll hae to gang roond by Gledsmuir Brig, and that's twenty mile o' a differ. 'Deed, it's no like that Sandy Jamieson will get a guid price the morn for sic sair forfochen beasts."

Then with firmly gripped staff he marched stoutly into the tide till it ran hissing below his armpits. "I could dae 't alane," he cried, "but no wi' a burden. For, losh, if ye slippit, ye 'd be in the Manor Pool afore ye could draw breath."

And so we waited with the great white droves and five angry men beyond, and the path blocked by a surging flood. For half an hour we waited, holding anxious consultation across the stream, when to us thus busied there entered a newcomer, a helper from the ends of the earth.

He was a man of something over middle size, but with a stoop forward that shortened him to something beneath it. His dress was ragged homespun, the cast-off clothes of some sportsman, and in his arms he bore a bundle of sticks and heather-roots which marked his calling. I knew him for a tramp who long had wandered in the place, but I could not account for the whole-voiced shout of greeting which met him as he stalked down the path. He lifted his eyes and looked solemnly and long at the scene. Then something of delight came into his eye, his face relaxed, and flinging down his burden, he stripped his coat and came toward us.

"Come on, Yeddie, ye're sair needed," said the shepherd, and I watched with amazement this grizzled, crooked man seize a sheep by the fleece and drag it to the water. Then he was in the midst, stepping warily, now up, now down the channel, but always nearing the farther bank. At last with a final struggle he landed his charge, and turned to journey back. Fifteen times did he cross that water, and at the end his mean figure had wholly changed. For now he was straighter and stronger, his eye flashed, and his voice, as he cried out to the drovers, had in it a tone of command. I marvelled at the transformation; and when at length

117

he had donned once more his ragged coat and shouldered his bundle, I asked the shepherd his name.

"They ca' him Adam Logan," said my friend, his face still bright with excitement, "but maist folk ca' him 'Streams o' Water'."

"Ay," said I, "and why 'Streams of Water'?"

"Juist for the reason ye see," said he.

"Now I knew the shepherd's way, and I held my peace, for it was clear that his mind was revolving other matters, concerned most probably with the high subject of the morrow's prices. But in a little, as we crossed the moor toward his dwelling, his thoughts relaxed and he remembered my question. So he answered me thus –

"Oh, ay; as ye were sayin', he's a queer man, Yeddie – aye been; guid kens whaur he cam frae first, for he's been trampin' the countryside since ever I mind, and that's no yesterday. He maun be sixty year, and yet he's as fresh as ever. If onything, he's a thocht dafter in his ongaein's, mair silent-like. But ye'll hae heard tell o' him afore?"

I owned ignorance.

"Tut," said he, "ye ken nocht. But Yeddie had aye a queer crakin' for waters. He never gangs on the road. Wi' him it's juist up yae glen and doon anither, and aye keepin' by the burnside. He kens every water i' the warld, every bit sheuch and burnie frae Gallowa' to Berwick. And then he kens the way o' spates the best I ever saw, and I've heard tell o' him fordin' waters when nae ither thing could leeve i' them. He can weyse and wark his road sae cunnin'ly on the stanes that the roughest flood, if it's no juist fair ower his heid, canna upset him. Mony a sheep has he saved to me, and it's mony a guid drove wad never hae won to Gledsmuir market but for Yeddie."

I listened with a boy's interest in any romantic narration. Somehow, the strange figure wrestling in the brown stream took fast hold on my mind, and I asked the shepherd for farther tales.

"There's little mair to tell," he said, "for a gangrel life is nane the liveliest. But d' ye ken the lang-nebbit hill which cocks its tap abune the Clachlands heid? Weel, he's got a wee bit o' grund on the tap frae the Yerl, and there he's howkit a grave for himsel'. He's sworn me and twae-three ithers to bury him there, wherever he may dee. It's a queer fancy in the auld dotterel."

So the shepherd talked, and as at evening we stood by his door we saw a figure moving into the gathering shadows. I knew it at once, and did not need my friend's, "There gangs 'Streams o' Water'," to recognise it. Something wild and pathetic in the old man's face haunted me like a dream, and as the dusk swallowed him up, he seemed like some old Druid recalled of the gods to his ancient habitation of the moors.

II

Two years passed, and April came with her suns and rains, and again the waters brimmed full in the valleys. Under the clear, shining sky the lambing went on, and the faint bleat of sheep brooded on the hills. In a land of young heather and green upland meads, of faint odours of moor-burn, and hilltops falling in lone ridges to the skyline, the veriest St Anthony would not abide indoors; so I flung all else to the winds and went a-fishing.

At the first pool on the Callowa, where the great flood sweeps nobly round a ragged shoulder of hill, and spreads into broad deeps beneath a tangle of birches, I began my toils. The turf was still wet with dew and the young leaves gleamed in the glow of morning. Far up the stream rose the terrible hills which hem the mosses and tarns of that tableland, whence flow the greater waters of the countryside. An ineffable freshness, as of the morning alike of the day and the seasons, filled the clear hill air, and the remote peaks gave the needed touch of intangible romance.

119

But as I fished, I came on a man sitting in a green dell, busy at the making of brooms. I knew his face and dress, for who could forget such eclectic raggedness? – and I remembered that day two years before when he first hobbled into my ken. Now, as I saw him there, I was captivated by the nameless mystery of his appearance. There was something startling to one, accustomed to the lacklustre gaze of town-bred folk, in the sight of an eye as keen and wild as a hawk's from sheer solitude and lonely travelling. He was so bent and scarred with weather that he seemed as much a part of that woodland place as the birks themselves, and the noise of his labours did not startle the birds which hopped on the branches.

Little by little I won his acquaintance – by a chance reminiscence, a single tale, the mention of a friend. Then he made me free of his knowledge, and my fishing fared well that day. He dragged me up little streams to sequestered pools, where I had astonishing success; and then back to some great swirl in the Callowa where he had seen monstrous takes. And all the while he delighted me with his talk, of men and things, of weather and place, pitched high in his thin, old voice, and garnished with many tones of lingering sentiment. He spoke in a broad, slow Scots, with so quaint a lilt in his speech that one seemed to be in an elder time among people of a quieter life and a quainter kindliness.

Then by chance I asked him of a burn of which I had heard, and how it might be reached. I shall never forget the tone of his answer as his face grew eager and he poured forth his knowledge.

"Ye'll gang up the Knowe Burn, which comes down into the Cauldshaw. It's a wee tricklin' thing, trowin' in and out o' pools i' the rock, and comin' doun out o' the side o' Caerfraun. Yince a merrymaiden bided there, I've heard folks say, and used to win the sheep frae the Cauldshaw herd, and bile them i' the muckle pool below the fa'. They say that there's a road to the Ill Place there, and when the Deil likit he sent up the lowe and garred the water faem and fizzle like an auld kettle. But if ye've gaun to the Colm Burn ye maun haud atower the rig o' the hill frae the Knowe heid, and ye'll come to it wimplin' among green brae faces. It's a bonny bit, rale lonesome, but awfu' bonny, and there's mony braw trout in its siller flows."

Then I remembered all I had heard of the old man's craze, and I humoured him.

"It's a fine countryside for burns," I said.

"Ye may say that," said he, gladly, "a weel-watered land. But a' this braw south country is the same. I've traivelled frae the Yeavering Hill in the Cheviots to the Caldons in Galloway, and it's a' the same. When I was young, I've seen me gang north to the Hielands and doun to the English lawlands, but now that I'm gettin' auld, I maun bide i' the yae place. There's no a burn in the South I dinna ken, and I never cam to the water I couldna ford."

"No?" said I. "I've seen you at the ford o' Clachlands in' the Lammas floods."

"Often I've been there," he went on, speaking like one calling up vague memories. "Yince, when Tam Rorison was drooned, honest man. Yince again, when the brigs were ta'en awa', and the Back House o' Clachlands had nae bread for a week. But O, Clachlands is a bit easy water. But I've seen the muckle Aller come roarin' sae high that it washed awa' a sheepfold that stood weel up on the hill. And I've seen this verra burn, this bonny clear Callowa, lyin' like a loch for miles i' the haugh. But I never heeds a spate, for if a man just kens the way o't it's a canny, hairmless thing. I couldna wish to dee better than just be happit i' the waters o' my ain countryside, when my legs fail and I'm ower auld for the trampin'."

Something in that queer figure in the setting of the hills struck a note of curious pathos. And towards evening as we returned down the glen the note grew keener. A spring sunset of gold and crimson flamed in our backs and turned the clear pools to fire. Far off down the vale the plains and the sea gleamed half in shadow.

Somehow in the fragrance and colour and the delectable crooning of the stream, the fantastic and the dim seemed tangible and present, and high sentiment revelled for once in my prosaic heart.

And still more in the breast of my companion. He stopped and sniffed the evening air, as he looked far over hill and dale and then back to the great hills above us. "Yon's Crappel, and Caerdon and the Laigh Law," he said, lingering with relish over each name, "and the Gled comes doun atween them. I haena been there for a twalmonth, and I maun hae anither glisk o't, for it's a braw place." And then some bitter thought seemed to seize him, and his mouth twitched. "I'm an auld man," he cried, "and I canna see ye a' again. There's burns and mair burns in the high hills that I'll never win to." Then he remembered my presence, and stopped. "Ye maun excuse me," he said huskily, "but the sicht o' a' thae lang blue hills makes me daft, now that I've faun i' the vale o' years. Yince I was young and could get where I wantit, but now I am auld and maun bide i' the same bit. And I'm aye thinkin' o' the waters I've been to, and the green heichs and howes and the bricht pools that I canna win to again. I maun e'en be content wi' the Callowa, which is as bonny as the best."

And then I left him, wandering down by the streamside and telling his crazy meditations to himself.

III

A space of years elapsed ere I met him, for fate had carried me far from the upland valleys. But once again I was afoot on the white moor roads; and, as I swung along one autumn afternoon up the path which leads from the Glen of Callowa to the Gled, I saw a figure before me which I knew for my friend. When I overtook him, his appearance puzzled and vexed me. Age seemed to have come on him at a bound, and in the tottering figure and the stoop of weakness I had difficulty in recognising the hardy frame of the man as I had known him. Something, too, had come over his face. His brow was clouded, and the tan of weather stood out hard and cruel on a blanched cheek. His eye seemed both wilder and sicklier, and for the first time I saw him with none of the appurtenances of his trade.

He greeted me feebly and dully, and showed little wish to speak. He walked with slow, uncertain step, and his breath laboured with a new panting. Every now and then he would look at me sidewise, and in his feverish glance I could detect none of the free kindliness of old. The man was ill in body and mind.

I asked him how he had done since I saw him last.

"It's an ill world now," he said in a slow, querulous voice. "There's nae need for honest men, and nae leevin'. Folk dinna care for me ava now. They dinna buy my besoms, they winna let me bide a' nicht in their byres, and they're no like the kind canty folk in the auld times. And a' the countryside is changin'. Doun by Goldieslaw they're makkin' a dam for takin' water to the toun, and they're thinkin' o' daein' the like wi' the Callowa. Guid help us, can they no let the works o' God alane? Is there no room for them in the dirty lawlands that they maun file the hills wi' their biggins?"

I conceived dimly that the cause of his wrath was a scheme for waterworks at the border of the uplands, but I had less concern for this than his strangely feeble health.

"You are looking ill," I said. "What has come over you?"

"Oh, I canna last for aye," he said mournfully. "My auld body's about dune. I've warkit ower sair when I had it, and it's gaun to fail on my hands. Sleepin' out o' wat nichts and gangin' lang wantin' meat are no the best ways for a long life;" and he smiled the ghost of a smile.

And then he fell to wild telling of the ruin of the place and the hardness of the people, and I saw that want and bare living had gone far to loosen his wits. I knew the countryside with the knowledge of many years, and I recognised that change was only in his mind. And a great pity seized me for this lonely figure toiling on in the bitterness of regret. I tried to comfort him, but my words were useless, for he took no heed of me; with bent head and faltering step he mumbled his sorrows to himself.

Then of a sudden we came to the crest of the ridge where the road dips from the hilltop to the sheltered valley. Sheer from the heather ran the white streak till it lost itself among the reddening rowans and the yellow birks of the wood. All the land was rich in autumn colour, and the shining waters dipped and fell through a pageant of russet and gold. And all around hills huddled in silent spaces, long brown moors crowned with cairns, or steep fortresses of rock and shingle rising to foreheads of steel-like grey. The autumn blue faded in the far skyline to white, and lent distance to the farther peaks. The hush of the wilderness, which is far different from the hush of death, brooded over the scene, and like faint music came the sound of a distant scythe-swing, and the tinkling whisper which is the flow of a hundred streams.

I am an old connoisseur in the beauties of the uplands, but I held my breath at the sight. And when I glanced at my companion, he, too, had raised his head, and stood with wide nostrils and gleaming eye revelling in this glimpse of Arcady. Then he found his voice, and the weakness and craziness seemed for one moment to leave him.

"It's my ain land," he cried, "and I'll never leave it. D' ye see yon broun hill wi' the lang cairn?" and he gripped my arm fiercely and directed my gaze. "Yon's my bit. I howkit it richt on the verra tap, and ilka year I gang there to mak it neat and orderly. I've trystit wi' fower men in different pairishes, that whenever they hear o' my death, they'll cairry me up yonder and bury me there. And then I'll never leave it, but lie still and quiet to the warld's end. I'll aye hae the sound o' water in my ear, for there's five burns tak' their rise on that hillside, and on a' airts the glens gang doun to the Gled and the Aller. I'll hae a brawer buryin' than ony, for a hilltop's better than a dowie kirkyaird."

Then his spirit failed him, his voice sank, and he was almost the feeble gangrel once more. But not yet, for again his eye swept the ring of hills, and he muttered to himself names which I knew for streams, lingeringly, lovingly, as of old affections. "Aller and Gled and Callowa," he crooned, "braw names, and Clachlands and Cauldshaw and the Lanely Water. And I maunna forget the Stark and the Lin and the bonny streams o' the Creran. And what mair? I canna mind a' the burns, the Howe and the Hollies and the Fawn and the links o' the Manor. What says the Psalmist about them?

> "Like streams o' water in the South
> Our bondage, Lord, recall."

Ay, but that's the name for them. 'Streams o' water in the South.' "

And as we went down the slopes to the darkening vale I heard him crooning to himself in a high, quavering voice the single distich; then in a little his weariness took him again, and he plodded on with no thought save for his sorrows.

IV

The conclusion of this tale belongs not to me but to the shepherd of the Redswirehead, and I heard it from him in his dwelling, as I stayed the night, belated on the darkening moors. He told me it after supper in a flood of misty Doric, and his voice grew rough at times, and he poked viciously at the dying peat.

"In the last back end I was at Gledfoot wi' sheep, and a weary job I had and little credit. Ye ken the place, a lang dreich shore wi' the wind swirlin' and bitin' to the bane, and the broun Gled water choked wi' Solloway sand. There was nae room in ony inn in the town, so I made good to gang to a bit public on the Harbour Walk, where sailor-folk and fishermen feucht and drank, and nae dacent men frae the hills thocht of gangin'. I was in a

125

gey ill way, for I had sell't my beasts dooms cheap, and I thocht o' the lang miles hame in the wintry weather. So after a bite o' meat I gangs out to get the air and clear my heid, which was a' rammled wi' the auction ring.

"And whae did I find, sittin' on a bench at the door, but the auld man Yeddie. He was waur changed than ever. His lang hair was hingin' ower his broo, and his face was thin and white as a ghaist's. His claes fell loose about him, and he sat wi' his hand on his auld stick and his chin on his hand, hearin' nocht and glowerin' afore him. He never saw nor kenned me till I shook him by the shoulders, and cried him by his name.

" 'Whae are ye?' says he, in a thin voice that gaed to my hert.

" 'Ye ken me fine, ye auld fule,' says I. 'I'm Jock Rorison o' the Redswirehead, whaur ye've stoppit often.'

" 'Redswirehead,' he says, like a man in a dream, 'Redswirehead! That's at the tap o' the Clachlands Burn as ye gang ower to the Dreichil.'

" 'And what are ye daein' here? It's no your countryside ava, and ye're no fit noo for lang trampin'.'

" 'No,' says he, in the same weak voice and wi' nae fushion in him, 'but they winna hae me up yonder noo. I'm ower auld and useless. Yince a'body was gled to see me, and wad keep me as lang's I wantit, and had aye a guid word at meeting and pairting. Noo it's a' changed, and my wark's dune.'

"I saw fine that the man was daft, but what answer could I gie to his havers? Folk in the Callowa Glens are as kind as afore, but ill weather and auld age had put queer notions intil his heid. Forbye, he was seeck, seeck unto death, and I saw mair in his ee than I likit to think.

" 'Come in by and get some meat, man,' I said. 'Ye're famishin' wi' cauld and hunger.'

" 'I canna eat,' he says, and his voice never changed. 'It's lang since I had a bite, for I'm no hungry. But I'm awfu' thirsty. I cam here yestereen, and I can get nae water to drink like the water in the hills. I maun be settin' out back the morn, if the Lord spares me.'

"I mindit fine that the body wad tak nae drink like an honest man, but maun aye draibble wi' burn water, and noo he had got the thing on the brain. I never spak a word, for the maitter was bye ony mortal's aid.

"For lang he sat quiet. Then he lifts his heid and looks awa ower the grey sea. A licht for a moment cam intil his een.

" 'Whatna big water's that?' he said, wi' his puir mind aye rinnin' on waters.

" 'That's the Solloway,' says I.

" 'The Solloway,' says he; 'it's a big water, and it wad be an ill job to ford it.'

" 'Nae man ever fordit it,' I said.

" 'But I never yet cam to the water I couldna ford,' says he. 'But what's that queer smell i' the air? Something snell and cauld and unfreendly, no like the reek o' bogs and hills.'

" 'That's the salt, for we're at the sea here, the mighty ocean.'

"He keepit repeatin' the word ower in his mouth. 'The salt, the salt, I've heard tell o' it afore, but I dinna like it. It's terrible cauld and unhamely.'

"By this time an onding o' rain was comin' up frae the water, and I bade the man come indoors to the fire. He followed me, as biddable as a sheep, draggin' his legs like yin far gone in seeckness. I set him by the fire, and put whisky at his elbow, but he wadna touch it.

" 'I've nae need o' it,' said he. 'I'm fine and warm;' and he sits staring at the fire, aye comin' ower again and again, 'The Solloway, the Solloway. It's a guid name and a muckle water.' But sune I gaed to my bed, being heavy wi' sleep, for I had traivelled for twae days."

"The next morn I was up at six and out to see the weather. It was a' changed. The muckle tides lay lang and still as our ain Loch o'

127

the Lee, and far ayont I saw the big blue hills o' England shine bricht and clear. I thankit Providence for the day, for it was better to tak the lang miles back in sic a sun than in a blast of rain.

"But as I lookit I saw some folk comin' up frae the beach cairryin' something atween them. My hert gied a loup, and 'some puir, drooned sailor-body,' says I to mysel', 'whae has perished in yesterday's storm.' But as they came nearer I got a glisk which made me run like daft, and lang ere I was up on them I saw it was Yeddie.

"He lay drippin' and white, wi' his puir auld hair lyin' back frae his broo and his duds clingin' to the legs. But out o' the face there seemed to have gone a' the seeckness and weariness. His een were stelled, as if he had been lookin' forrit to something, and his lips were set like a man on a lang errand. And mair, his stick was grippit sae firm in his hand that nae man could loose it, so they e'en let it be.

"Then they tellt me the tale o' 't, how at the earliest licht they had seen him wanderin' alang the sands, juist as they were putting out their boats to sea. They wondered and watched him, till of a sudden he turned to the water and wadit in, keepin' straucht on till he was oot o' sicht. They rowed a' their pith to the place, but they were ower late. Yince they saw his heid appear abune water, still wi' his face to the ither side; and then they got his body, for the tide was rinnin' low in the mornin'. I tell 't them a' I kenned o' him and they were sair affected. 'Puir cratur,' said yin, 'he's shürely better now.'

"So we brocht him up to the house and laid him there till the folk i' the town had heard o' the death. Syne I got a wooden coffin made and put him in it, juist as he was, wi' his staff in his hand and his auld duds about him. I mindit o' my sworn word, for I was yin o' the four that had promised, and I ettled to dae his bidding. It was three-and-twenty mile to the hills, and thirty to the lanely tap whaur he had howkit his grave. But I never heedit it. I'm a strong man, weel-used to the walkin', and my hert was sair for the puir auld man I had kenned sae well. Now that he had gotten deliverance from his affliction, it was mine to leave him in the place he wantit. Forbye he wasna muckle heavier than a bairn.

"It was a long road, a sair road, but I did it, and by seven o'clock I was at the edge o' the muirlands. There was a braw mune, and a' the glens and taps stood out as clear as midday. Bit by bit, for I was gey tired, I warstled ower the rigs and up the cleuchs to the Gled-head, syne up the stany Gled-cleuch to the lang grey hill which they ca' the Hurlybackit. By ten I had come to the cairn, and black i' the yellow licht I saw the grave. So there I buried him, and though I'm no a releegious man, I couldna help sayin' ower him the guid words o' the Psalmist,

> " 'Like streams of water in the South
> Our bondage, Lord, recall.' "

This was the shepherd's tale, and I heard it out in silence.

So if you go from the Gled to the Aller, and keep far over the north side of the Muckle Muneraw, you will come in time to a stony ridge which ends in a cairn. There you will see the whole hill country of the south, a hundred lochs, a myriad streams, and a forest of hilltops. There on the very crest lies the old man, in the heart of his own land, at the fountainhead of his many waters. If you listen you will hear a hushed noise as of the swaying in trees or a ripple on the sea. It is the sound of the rising of burns, which, innumerable and unnumbered, flow thence to the silent glens for evermore.

129

THE MOOR-SONG

THE TALE OF THE RESPECTABLE WHAUP AND THE GREAT GODLY MAN

This is a story that I heard from the King of the Numidians, who with his tattered retinue encamps behind the peat-ricks. If you ask me where and when it happened I fear that I am scarce ready with an answer. But I will vouch my honour for its truth; and if anyone seek further proof, let him go east the town and west the town and over the fields of Noman'sland to the Long Muir, and if he find not the King there among the peat-ricks, and get not a courteous answer to his question, then times have changed in that part of the country, and he must continue the quest to His Majesty's castle in Spain.

Once upon a time, says the tale, there was a Great Godly Man, a shepherd to trade, who lived in a cottage among heather. If you looked east in the morning, you saw miles of moor running wide to the flames of sunrise, and if you turned your eyes west in the evening, you saw a great confusion of dim peaks with the dying eye of the sun set in a crevice. If you looked north, too, in the afternoon, when the life of the day is near its end and the world grows wise, you might have seen a country of low hills and haughlands with many waters running sweet among meadows. But if you looked south in the dusty forenoon or at hot midday, you saw the far-off glimmer of a white road, the roofs of the ugly little clachan of Kilmaclavers, and the rigging of the fine new kirk of Threepdaidle.

It was a Sabbath afternoon in the hot weather, and the man had been to kirk all the morning. He had heard a grand sermon from the minister (or it may have been the priest, for I am not sure of the date and the King told the story quickly) – a fine discourse with fifteen heads and three parentheses. He held all the parentheses and fourteen of the heads in his memory, but he had forgotten the fifteenth; so for the purpose of recollecting it, and also for the sake of a walk, he went forth in the afternoon into the open heather. The air was mild and cheering, and with an even step he strolled over the turf and into the deeps of the moor.

The whaups were crying everywhere, making the air hum like the twanging of a bow. *Poo-eelie, Poo-eelie,* they cried, *Kirlew, Kirlew, Whaup, Wha-up.* Sometimes they came low, all but brushing him, till they drove settled thoughts from his head. Often had he been on the moors, but never had he seen such a stramash among the feathered clan. The wailing iteration vexed him, and he *shoo'd* the birds away with his arms. But they seemed to mock him and whistle in his very face, and at the flaff of their wings his heart grew sore. He waved his great stick; he picked up bits of loose moor-rock and flung them wildly; but the godless crew paid never a grain of heed. The morning's sermon was still in his head, and the grave words of the minister still rattled in his ear, but he could get no comfort for this intolerable piping. At last his patience failed him and he swore unchristian words. "Deil rax the birds' thrapples," he cried.

At this all the noise was hushed and in a twinkling the moor was empty. Only one bird was left, standing on tall legs before him with its head bowed upon its breast, and its beak touching the heather.

Then the man repented his words and stared at the thing in the moss. "What bird are ye?" he asked thrawnly.

"I am a Respectable Whaup," said the bird, "and I kenna why ye have broken in on our family gathering. Once in a hundred years we foregather for decent conversation, and here we are interrupted by a muckle, sweerin' man."

Now the shepherd was a fellow of great sagacity, yet he never thought it a queer thing that he should be having talk in the mid-moss with a bird. Truth, he had no mind on the matter.

"What for were ye making siccan a din, then?" he asked. "D' ye no ken ye were disturbing the afternoon of the holy Sabbath?"

The bird lifted its eyes and regarded him solemnly. "The Sabbath is a day of rest and gladness," it said, "and is it no reasonable that we should enjoy the like?"

The shepherd shook his head, for the presumption staggered him. "Ye little ken what ye speak of," he said. "The Sabbath is for them that have the chance of salvation, and it has been decreed that Salvation is for Adam's race and no for the beasts that perish."

The whaup gave a whistle of scorn. "I have heard all that long ago. In my great grandmother's time, which 'ill be a thousand years and mair syne, there came a people from the south with bright brass things on their heads and breasts and terrible swords at their thighs. And with them were some lang-gowned men who kenned the stars and would come out o' nights to talk to the deer and the corbies in their ain tongue. And one, I mind, foregathered with my great-grandmother and told her that the souls o' men flitted in the end to braw meadows where the gods bide or gaed down to the black pit which they ca' Hell. But the souls o' birds, he said, die wi' their bodies and that's the end o' them. Likewise in my mother's time, when there was a great abbey down yonder by the Threepdaidle Burn which they called the House of Kilmaclavers, the auld monks would walk out in the evening to pick herbs for their distillings, and some were wise and kenned the ways of bird and beast. They would crack often o' nights with my ain family, and tell them that Christ had saved the souls o' men, but that birds and beasts were perishable as the dew o' heaven. And now ye have a black-gowned man in

Threepdaidle who threeps on the same owercome. Ye may a' ken something o' your ain kitchen-midden, but certes! ye ken little o' the warld beyond it."

Now this angered the man, and he rebuked the bird. "These are great mysteries," he said, "which are no to be mentioned in the ears of an unsanctified creature. What can a thing like you wi' a lang neb and twae legs like stilts ken about the next warld?"

"Weel, weel," said the whaup, "we'll let the matter be. Everything to its ain trade, and I will not dispute with ye on metapheesics. But if ye ken something about the next warld, ye ken terrible little about this."

Now this angered the man still more, for he was a shepherd reputed to have great skill in sheep and esteemed the nicest judge of hogg and wether in all the countryside. "What ken ye about that?" he asked. "Ye may gang east to Yetholm and west to Kells, and no find a better herd."

"If sheep were a'," said the bird, "ye micht be right; but what o' the wide warld and the folk in it? Ye are Simon Etterick o' the Lowe Moss. Do ye ken aucht o' your forbears?"

"My father was a God-fearing man at the Kennel-head, and my grandfather and great-grandfather afore him. One o' our name, folk say, was shot at a dyke-back by the Black Westeraw."

"If that's a'," said the bird, "ye ken little. Have ye never heard o' the little man, the fourth back from yoursel', who killed the Miller o' Bewcastle at the Lammas Fair? That was in my ain time, and from my mother I have heard o' the Covenanter, who got a bullet in his wame hunkering behind the divot-dyke and praying to his Maker. There were others o' your name rode in the Hermitage forays and burned Naworth and Warkworth and Castle Gay. I have heard o' an Etterick, Sim o' the Redcleuch, who cut the throat o' Jock Johnson in his ain house by the Annan side. And my grandmother had tales o' auld Ettericks who rade wi' Douglas and the Bruce and the ancient Kings o' Scots; and she used to tell o' others in her mother's time, terrible shock-headed men, hunting the deer and rinnin' on the high moors, and bidin' in the broken stane biggings on the hilltaps."

The shepherd stared, and he, too, saw the picture. He smelled the air of battle and lust and foray, and forgot the Sabbath.

"And you yoursel'," said the bird, "are sair fallen off from the auld stock. Now ye sit and spell in books, and talk about what ye little understand, when your fathers were roaming the warld. But little cause have I to speak, for I too am a downcome. My bill is two inches shorter than my mother's, and my grandmother was taller on her feet. The warld is getting weaklier things to dwell in it, ever since I mind mysel'."

"Ye have the gift o' speech, bird," said the man, "and I would hear mair." You will perceive that he had no mind of the Sabbath day or the fifteenth head of the forenoon's discourse.

"What things have I to tell ye when ye dinna ken the very horn-book o' knowledge? Besides, I am no clatter-vengeance to tell stories in the middle o' the muir, where there are ears open high and low. There's others than me wi' mair experience and a better skill at the telling. Our clan was well acquaint wi' the reivers and lifters o' the muirs, and could crack fine o' wars and the taking of cattle. But the blue hawk that lives in the corrie o' the Dreichil can speak o' kelpies and the dwarfs that bide in the hill. The heron, the lang solemn fellow, kens o' the greenwood fairies and the wood elfins, and the wild geese that squatter on the tap o' the Muneraw will croak to ye of the merrymaidens and the girls o' the pool. The wren – he that hops in the grass below the birks – has the story of the *Lost Ladies of the Land*, which is ower auld and sad for any but the wisest to hear; and there is a wee bird bide in the heather – hill-lintie men call him – who sings the *Lay of the West Wind*, and the *Glee of the Rowan Berries*. But what am I talking of? What are these things to you, if ye have not first heard the Moor-song, which is the beginning and end o' all things?"

"I have heard no songs," said the man, "save the sacred psalms o' God's Kirk."

"Bonny sangs," said the bird. "Once I flew by the hinder end o' the Kirk and I keekit in. A wheen auld wives wi' mutches and a wheen solemn men wi' hoasts! Be sure the Moor-song is no like yon."

"Can ye sing it, bird?" said the man, "for I am keen to hear it."

"Me sing," cried the bird, "me that has a voice like a craw! Na, na, I canna sing it, but maybe I can tak ye where ye may hear it. When I was young an auld bog-blitter did the same to me, and sae began my education. But are ye willing and brawly willing? – for if ye get but a sough of it ye will never mair have an ear for other music."

"I am willing and brawly willing," said the man.

"Then meet me at the Gled's Cleuch Head at the sun's setting," said the bird, and it flew away.

Now it seemed to the man that in a twinkling it was sunset, and he found himself at the Gled's Cleuch Head with the bird flapping in the heather before him. The place was a long rift in the hill, made green with juniper and hazel, where it was said True Thomas came to drink the water.

"Turn ye to the west," said the whaup, "and let the sun fall on your face, then turn ye five times round about and say after me the Rune of the Heather and the Dew." And before he knew, the man did as he was told, and found himself speaking strange words, while his head hummed and danced as if in a fever.

"Now lay ye down and put your ear to the earth," said the bird, and the man did so. Instantly a cloud came over his brain, and he did not feel the ground on which he lay or the keen hill air which blew about him. He felt himself falling deep into an abysm of space, then suddenly caught up and set among the stars of heaven. Then slowly from the stillness there welled forth music, drop by drop like the clear falling of rain, and the man shuddered, for he knew that he heard the beginning of the Moor-song.

High rose the air, and trembled among the tallest pines and the summits of great hills. And in it were the sting of rain and the blatter of hail, the soft crush of snow and the rattle of thunder among crags. Then it quieted to the low sultry croon which told of blazing midday when the streams are parched and the bent crackles like dry tinder. Anon it was evening, and the melody dwelled among the high soft notes which mean the coming of dark and the green light of sunset. Then the whole changed to a great paean which rang like an organ through the earth. There were trumpet notes in it and flute notes and the plaint of pipes. "Come forth," it cried; "the sky is wide and it is a far cry to the world's end. The fire crackles fine o' nights below the firs, and the smell of roasting meat and woodsmoke is dear to the heart of man. Fine, too, is the sting of salt and the risp of the north wind in the sheets. Come forth, one and all, to the great lands oversea, and the strange tongues and the fremit peoples. Learn before you die to follow the Piper's Son, and though your old bones bleach among grey rocks, what matter, if you have had your bellyful of life and come to the land of Heart's Desire?" And the tune fell low and witching, bringing tears to the eyes and joy to the heart; and the man knew (though no one told him) that this was the first part of the Moor-song, the *Song of the Open Road*, the *Lilt of the Adventurer*, which shall be now and ever and to the end of days.

Then the melody changed to a fiercer and sadder note. He saw his forefathers, gaunt men and terrible, run stark among woody hills. He heard the talk of the bronze-clad invader, and the jar and clangour as flint met steel. Then rose the last coronach of his own people, hiding in wild glens, starving in corries, or going hopelessly to the death. He heard the cry of Border foray, the shouts of the poor Scots as they harried Cumberland, and he himself rode in the midst of them. Then the tune fell more mournful and slow, and Flodden lay before him. He saw the flower of Scots gentry around their king, gashed to the breastbone, still fronting the lines of the south, though the paleness of death sat on each forehead. "The flowers of the Forest are gone," cried the lilt, and through the long years he heard the cry of the lost, the desperate, fighting for kings over the water and princes in the heather. "Who cares?" cried the air. "Man must die, and how can he die better than in the stress of fight with his heart high and alien blood on his sword? Heigh-ho! One against twenty, a child against a host, this is the romance of life." And the man's heart swelled, for he knew (though no one told him) that this was the *Song of Lost Battles*, which only the great can sing before they die.

But the tune was changing, and at the change the man shivered, for the air ran up to the high notes and then down to the deeps with an eldritch cry, like a hawk's scream at night, or a witch's song in the gloaming. It told of those who seek and never find, the quest that knows no fulfilment. "There is a road," it cries, "which leads to the Moon and the Great Waters. No changehouse cheers it, and it has no end; but it is a fine road, a braw road – who will follow it?" And the man knew (though no one told him) that this was the *Ballad of Grey Weather*, which makes him who hears it sick all the days of his life for something which he cannot name. It is the song which the birds sing on the moor in the autumn nights, and the old crow on the treetop hears and flaps his wing. It is the lilt which old men and women hear in the darkening of their days, and sigh for the unforgetable; and lovesick girls get catches of it and play pranks with their lovers. It is a song so old that Adam heard it in the Garden before Eve came to comfort him, so young that from it still flows the whole joy and sorrow of earth.

Then it ceased, and all of a sudden the man was rubbing his eyes on the hillside, and watching the falling dusk. "I have heard the Moor-song," he said to himself, and he walked home in a daze. The whaups were crying, but none came near him, though he looked hard for the bird that had spoken with him. It may be that it was there and he did not know it, or it may be that the whole thing was only a dream; but of this I cannot say.

The next morning the man rose and went to the manse.

"I am glad to see you, Simon," said the minister, "for it will soon be the Communion Season, and it is your duty to go round with the tokens."

"True," said the man, "but it was another thing I came to talk about," and he told him the whole tale.

"There are but two ways of it, Simon," said the minister. "Either ye are the victim of witchcraft, or ye are a self-deluded man. If the former (whilk I am loth to believe), then it behoves ye to watch and pray lest ye enter into temptation. If the latter, then ye maun put a strict watch over a vagrom fancy, and ye'll be quit o' siccan whigmaleeries."

Now Simon was not listening, but staring out of the window. "There was another thing I had it in my mind to say," said he. "I have come to lift my lines, for I am thinking of leaving the place."

"And where would ye go?" asked the minister, aghast.

"I was thinking of going to Carlisle and trying my luck as a dealer, or maybe pushing on with droves to the South."

"But that's a cauld country where there are no faithfu' ministrations," said the minister.

"Maybe so, but I am not caring very muckle about ministrations," said the man, and the other looked after him in horror.

When he left the manse he went to a Wise Woman, who lived on the left side of the Kirkyard above Threepdaidle burn-foot. She was very old, and sat by the ingle day and night, waiting upon death. To her he told the same tale.

She listened gravely, nodding with her head. "Ach," she said, "I have heard a like story before. And where will you be going?"

"I am going south to Carlisle to try the dealing and droving," said the man, "for I have some skill of sheep."

"And will ye bide there?" she asked.

"Maybe aye, and maybe no," he said. "I had half a mind to push on to the big toun or even to the abroad. A man must try his fortune."

"That's the way of men," said the old wife. "I, too, have heard the Moor-song, and many women, who now sit decently spinning in Kilmaclavers, have heard it. But a woman may hear it and lay it up in her soul and bide at hame, while a man, if he get but a glisk of it in his fool's heart, must needs up and awa' to the warld's end on some daft-like ploy. But gang your ways and fare ye weel. My cousin Francie heard it, and he went north wi' a white cockade in his bonnet and a sword at his side, singing 'Charlie's come hame'. And Tam Crichtoun o' the Bourhopehead got a sough o' it one simmer's morning, and the last we heard o' Tam he was killed among the Frenchmen fechting like a fair deil. Once I heard a tinkler play a sprig of it on the pipes, and a' the lads were wud to follow him. Gang your ways, for I am near the end o' mine." And the old wife shook with her coughing.

So the man put up his belongings in a pack on his back and went whistling down the Great South Road.

Whether or not this tale has a moral it is not for me to say. The King (who told it me) said that it had, and quoted a scrap of Latin, for he had been at Oxford in his youth before he fell heir to his kingdom. One may hear tunes from the Moor-song, said he, in the thick of a storm on the scarp of a rough hill, in the low June weather, or in the sunset silence of a winter's night. But let none, he added, pray to have the full music, for it will make him who hears it a footsore traveller in the ways o' the world and a masterless man till death.

COMEDY IN THE FULL MOON

"I dislike that man," said Miss Phyllis, with energy.

"I have liked others better," said the Earl.

There was silence for a little as they walked up the laurelled path, which wound by hazel thicket and fir wood to the low ridges of moor.

"I call him Charles Surface," said Miss Phyllis again, with a meditative air. "I am no dabbler in the watercolours of character, but I think I could describe him."

"Try," said the Earl.

"Mr Charles Eden," began the girl, "is a man of talent. He has edged his way to fortune by dint of the proper enthusiasms and a seductive manner. He is a politician of repute and a lawyer of some practice, but his enemies say that like necessity he knows no law, and even his friends shrink from insisting upon his knowledge of politics. But he believes in all honest enthusiasms, temperance, land reform, and democracy with a capital D; he is, however, violently opposed to woman suffrage."

"Every man has his good points," murmured the Earl.

"You are interrupting me," said Miss Phyllis, severely. "To continue, his wife was the daughter of a baronet of ancient family and scanty means. Her husband supplied the element which she missed in her father's household, and today she is popular and her parties famous. Their house is commonly known as the Wilderness, because there the mixed multitude which came out of Egypt mingle with the chosen people. In character he is persuasive and

141

good-natured; but then good nature is really a vice which is called a virtue because it only annoys a man's enemies."

"I am learning a great deal tonight," said the man.

"You are," said Miss Phyllis. "But there, I have done. What I dislike in him is that one feels that he is the sort of man that has always lived in a house and is out of place anywhere but on a pavement."

"And you call this a sketch in watercolours?"

"No, indeed. In oils," said the girl, and they walked through a gate on to the short bent grass and the bouldered face of a hill. Something in the place seemed to strike her, for she dropped her voice and spoke simply.

"You know I am town-bred, but I am not urban in nature. I must chatter daily, but every now and then I grow tired of myself, and I hate people like Charles Eden who remind me of my weakness."

"Life," said the Earl, "may be roughly divided into – But there, it is foolish to be splitting up life by hairs on such a night."

Now they stood on the ridge's crest in the silver-grey light of a midsummer moon. Far up the long Gled valley they looked to the towering hills whence it springs; then to the left, where the sinuous Callowa wound its way beneath green and birk-clad mountains to the larger stream. In such a flood of brightness the far-distant peaks and shoulders stood out clear as day, but full of that hint of subtle and imperishable mystery with which the moon endows the great uplands in the height of summer. The air was still, save for the falling of streams and the twitter of nesting birds.

The girl stared wide-eyed at the scene, and her breath came softly with utter admiration.

"Oh, such a land!" she cried, "and I have never seen it before. Do you know I would give anything to explore these solitudes, and feel that I had made them mine. Will you take me with you?"

"But these things are not for you, little woman," he said. "You are too clever and smart and learned in the minutiae of human conduct. You would never learn their secret. You are too complex for simple, old-world life."

"Please don't say that," said Miss Phyllis, with pleading eyes. "Don't think so hardly of me. I am not all for show." Then with fresh wonder she looked over the wide landscape.

"Do you know these places?" she asked.

"I have wandered over them for ten years and more," said the Earl, "and I am beginning to love them. In other ten, perhaps, I shall have gone some distance on the road to knowledge. The best things in life take time and labour to reach."

The girl made no answer. She had found a little knoll in the opposite glen, clothed in a tangle of fern and hazels, and she eagerly asked its name.

"The folk here call it the Fairy Knowe," he said. "There is a queer story about it. They say that if any two people at midsummer in the full moon walk from the east and west so as to meet at the top, they will find a third there, who will tell them all the future. The old men speak of it carefully, but none believe it."

"Oh, let us go and try," said the girl, in glee. "It is quite early in the evening, and they will never miss us at home."

"But the others," said he.

"Oh, the others," with a gesture of amusement. "We left Mr Eden talking ideals to your mother, and the other men preparing for billiards. They won't mind."

"But it's more than half a mile, and you'll be very tired."

"No, indeed," said the girl, "I could walk to the top of the farthest hills tonight. I feel as light as a feather, and I do so want to know the future. It will be such a score to speak to my aunt with the prophetic accent of the things to be."

"Then come on," said the Earl, and the two went off through the heather.

II

If you walk into the inn kitchen at Callowa on a winter night, you will find it all but deserted, save for a chance traveller who is storm-stayed among the uncertain hills. Then men stay in their homes, for the place is little, and the dwellers in the remoter parts have no errand to town or village. But in the long nights of summer, when the moon is up and the hills dry underfoot, there are many folk down of an evening from the glens, and you may chance on men drinking a friendly glass with half a score of miles of journey before them. It is a cheerful scene – the wide room, with the twilight struggling with the new-lit lamp, the brown faces gathered around the table, and the rise and fall of the soft southern talk.

On this night you might have chanced on a special gathering, for it was the evening of the fair-day in Gled-foot, and many shepherds from the moors were eating their suppers and making ready for the road. It was then that Jock Rorison of the Redswirehead – known to all the world as Lang Jock to distinguish him from his cousin little Jock of the Nick o' the Hurlstanes – met his most ancient friend, the tailor of Callowa. They had been at school together, together they had suffered the pains of learning; and now the one's lot was cast at the back of Creation, and the other's in a little dark room in the straggling street of Callowa. A bottle celebrated their meeting, and there and then in the half-light of the gloaming they fell into talk. They spoke of friends and kin, and the toils of their life; of village gossip and market prices. Thence they drifted into vague moralisings and muttered exhortation in the odour of whisky. Soon they were amiable beyond their wont, praising each other's merit, and prophesying of good fortune. And then – alas for human nature! – there came the natural transition to argument and reviling.

"I wadna be you, Jock, for a thousand pounds," said the tailor. "Na, I wadna venture up that lang mirk glen o' yours for a' the wealth o' the warld."

"Useless body," said the shepherd, "and what for that?"

"Bide a' nicht here," said the tailor, "and step on in the mornin'. Man, ye're an auld freend, and I'm wae to think that aucht ill should befa' ye."

"Will ye no speak sense for yince, ye doited cratur?" was the ungracious answer, as the tall man rose to unhook his staff from the chimney corner. "I'm for stertin' if I'm to win hame afore mornin'."

"Weel," said the tailor, with the choked voice of the maudlin, "a' I've to say is that I wis the Lord may protect ye, for there's evil lurks i' the dens o' the way, saith the prophet."

"Stop, John Rorison, stop," again the tailor groaned. "O man, bethink ye o' your end."

"I wis ye wad bethink o' yin yoursel'."

The tailor heeded not the rudeness... "for ye ken a' the auld queer owercomes about the Gled Water. Yin Thomas the Rhymer made a word on 't. Quoth he,

> " 'By the Gled side
> The guid folk bide.' "

"Dodsake, Robin, ye're a man o' learnin' wi' your poetry," said the shepherd, with scorn. "Rhymin' about auld wives' havers, sic wark for a grown man!"

A vague recollection of wrath rose to the tailor's mind. But he answered with the laborious dignity of argument –

"I'm no sayin' that a' things are true that the body said. But I say this – that there's a heap o' queer things in the warld, mair nor you nor me nor onybody kens. Now, it's weel ken't that nane o' the folk about here like to gang to the Fairy Knowe..."

"It's weel ken't nae siccan thing," said the shepherd, rudely. "I wonder at you, a kirk member and an honest man's son, crakin' siccan blethers."

"I'm affirmin' naething," said the other, sententiously. "What I say is that nae man, woman, or child in this pairish, which is weel ken't for an intelligent yin, wad like to gang at the rising o' the mune up the side o' the Fairy Knowe. And it's weel ken't, tae, that when the twae daft lads frae the Rochan tried it in my faither's day and gaed up frae opposite airts, they met at the tap that which telled them a' that they ever did and a' that was ever like to befa' them, and put the fear o' deith on them for ever and ever. Mind, I'm affirmin' naething; but what think ye o' that?"

"I think this o' 't – that either the folk were mair fou than the Baltic or they were weak i' the heid afore ever they set out. But I'm tired o' hearin' a sensible man bletherin', so I'm awa' to the Redswirehead."

But the tailor was swollen with pride and romance, and filled with the audacity which comes from glasses replenished.

"Then I'll gang a bit o' the road wi' ye."

"And what for sae?" said the shepherd, darkly suspicious. Whisky drove care to his head, and made him the most irritable of friends.

"I want the air, and it's graund munelicht. Your road gangs by the Knowe, and we micht as weel mak the experiment. Mind ye, I'm affirmin' naething."

"Will ye no haud your tongue about what ye're affirmin'?"

"But I hold that it is a wise man's pairt to try all things, and whae kens but there micht be some queer sicht on that Knowe-tap? The auld folk were nane sae ready to be inventin' havers."

"I think the man's mad," was the shepherd's loud soliloquy. "You want me to gang and play daft-like pranks late at nicht among birks and stanes on a muckle knowe. Weel, let it be. It lies on my road hame, but ye 'd be weel serv't if some auld Druid cam out and grippit ye."

"Whae's bletherin' now," cried the tailor, triumphantly. "I dinna gang wi' ony supersteetions. I gang to get the fresh air and admire the wonderfu' works o' God. Hech, but they're bonny." And he waved a patronising finger to the moon.

The shepherd took him by the shoulder and marched him down the road. "Listen," said he, "I maun be hame afore the morn, and if ye're comin' wi' me ye'll hae to look smerter." So down the white path and over Gled bridge they took their way, two argumentative figures, clamouring in the silent, amber spaces of the night.

III

The farmer of the Lowe Moss was a choleric man at all times, but every now and again his temper failed him utterly. He was florid and full-blooded, and the hot weather drove him wild with discomfort. Then came the torments of a dusty market and completed the task; so it fell out that on that evening in June he drove home at a speed which bade fair to hurry him to a premature grave, and ate his supper with little thankfulness.

Then he reflected upon his manifold labours. The next day was the clipping, and the hill sheep would have to be brought down in the early morning. The shepherds would be at the folds by seven, and it would mean rising in the small hours to have the flocks in the low fields in time. Now his own shepherd was gone on an errand and would not be back till the morrow's breakfast. This meant that he, the wearied, the sorely tried, must be up with the lark and tramping the high pastures. The thought was too much for him. He could not face it. There would be no night's rest for his wearied legs, though the Lord knew how he needed it.

But as he looked through the window a thought grew upon his mind. He was tired and sore, but he might yet manage an hour or two of toil, if a sure prospect of rest lay at the end. The moon was up and bright, and he might gather the sheep to the low meadows as easily as in the morning. This would suffer him to sleep in peace to the hour of seven, which was indulgence indeed to one who habitually rose at five. He was a man of imagination and hope, who valued a prospect. Far better, he held, the present discomfort, if the certainty of ease lay before him. So he gathered his aching members, reached for his stick, whistled on his dogs, and set out.

It was a long climb up the ridges of the Lowe Burn to the stell of fir trees which marked his boundaries. Then began the gathering of the sheep, and a great scurry of dogs – black dots on the sleepy, moonlit hill. With much crying of master and barking of man the flocks were massed and turned athwart the slopes in the direction of the steading. All the while he limped grumblingly behind, thinking on bed, and leaving everything to his shaggy lieutenants. Then they crossed the Lowe Burn, skirted the bog, and came in a little to the lower meadows, while afar off over the rough crest of the Fairy Knowe twinkled the lights of the farm.

Meanwhile from another point of the hill there came another wayfarer to the same goal. The Sentimentalist was a picturesque figure on holiday, enjoying the summer in the way that still remains the best. Three weeks before he had flung the burden of work from his shoulders, and gone with his rod to the Callowa foot, whence he fished far and near even to the utmost recesses of the hills. On this evening the soft airs and the triumphant moon had brought him out of doors. He had a dim memory of a fragrant hazelled knoll above the rocky Gled, which looked up and down three valleys. The place drew him, as it lived in his memory, and he must needs get his plaid and cross the miles of heather to the wished-for sleeping place. There he would bide the night and see the sunrise, and haply the next morning make a raid into the near village to receive letters delayed for weeks.

He crossed the hill when the full white glory of the moon was already apparent in the valleys. The air was so still and mild that one might have slept there and then on the bare hillside and been no penny the worse. The heart of the Sentimentalist was cheered, and he scanned the prospect with a glad thankfulness. To think that three weeks ago he had been living in sultriness and dreary overwork, with a head as dazed as a spinning top and a ruin of nerves. Now every faculty was alive and keen, he had no thought of nerves, and his old Norfolk jacket, torn and easy, now stained with peat-water and now bleached with weather, was an index to his immediate past. In a little it would be all over, and then once more the dust and worry and heat. But meantime he was in fairyland, where there was little need for dreary prognostication.

And in truth it was a fairyland which dawned on his sight at the crest of the hill. A valley filled with hazy light, and in the middle darkly banded by the stream. All things, village, knoll, bog, and coppice, bright with a duskiness which revealed nought in detail, but only hints of form and colour. A noise of distant sheep rose from the sleeping place, and the single, solitary note of a night-bird far over the glen. At his foot were crushed thickets of little hill flowers, thyme and pansies and the odorous bog myrtle. Beneath him, not half a mile distant, was a mound with two lone birches on its summit, and he knew the place of his quest. This was the far-famed Fairy Knowe, where at midsummer the little folk danced, and where, so ran the tale, lay the mystic entrance, of which True Thomas spake, to the kingdom of dreams and shadows. Twenty-five miles distant a railway ran, but here there were still simplicity and antique tales. So in a fine spirit he set himself to the tangled meadowland which intervened.

IV

Miss Phyllis looked long and wonderingly at the tangled, moonlit hill. "Is this the place?" she asked.

The Earl nodded. "Do you feel devout, madam," said he, "and will you make the experiment?"

Miss Phyllis looked at him gravely. "Have I not scrambled over miles of bog, and do you think that I have risked my ankles for nothing? Besides I was always a devout believer."

"Then this is the way of it. You wait here and walk slowly up, while I will get to the other side. There is always a wonderful view at least on the top."

"But I am rather afraid that I..."

149

"Oh, very well," said the Earl. "If we don't perform our part, how can we expect a hard-worked goblin to do his?"

"Then," said Miss Phyllis, with tight lips and a sigh of melodrama, "lead on, my lord." And she watched his figure disappear with some misgiving.

For a little she scanned the patched shadow of birk and fern, and listened uneasily to the rustle of grasses. She heard the footsteps cease, and then rise again in the silence. Suddenly it seemed as if the place had come to life. A crackling, the noise of something in lumbering motion, came from every quarter. Then there would be a sound of scampering, and again the echo of heavy breathing. Now Miss Phyllis was not superstitious, and very little of a coward. Moreover, she was a young woman of the world, with a smattering of most things in heaven and earth, and the airs of an infinite experience. But this moonlit knoll, this wide-stretching, fantastic landscape, and the lucid glamour of the night, cast a spell on her, and for once she forgot everything. Miss Phyllis grew undeniably afraid.

She glanced timorously to the left, whence came the sounds, and then with commendable spirit began to climb the slope. If things were so queer she might reasonably carry out the letter of her injunctions, and in any case the Earl would be there to meet her. But the noise grew stranger, the sound of rustling and scrambling and breathing as if in the chase. Then to her amazement a crackle of twigs rose from her right, and as she hastily turned her head to meet the new alarum, she found herself face to face with a tall man in a plaid.

For one moment both stared in frank discomfiture. Miss Phyllis was horribly alarmed and in deepest mystery. But, she began to reflect, spirits have never yet been known to wear Norfolk jackets and knickerbockers, or take the guise of stalwart, brown-faced men. The Sentimentalist, too, after the natural surprise, recovered himself and held out his hand.

"How do you do, Miss Phyllis?" said he.

The girl gasped, and then a light of recognition came into her eyes.

"What are you doing here, Mr Grey?" she asked.

"Surely I have the first right to the question," the man said, smiling.

"Then, if you must know, I am looking for the customary spirit to tell the future. I thought you were the thing, and was fearfully scared."

"But who told you that story, Miss Phyllis? I did not think you would have been so credulous. Your part was always the acute critic's."

"Then you were wrong," said the girl, with emphasis. "Besides, it was Charlie Erskine's doing. He brought me here, and is faithfully keeping his compact at the other side of the hill."

"Well, well, Callowa had always a queer way of entertaining his guests. But there, Miss Phyllis, I have not seen civilisation for weeks, and am half inclined to believe in things myself. Never again shall you taunt me with ' boyish enthusiasm'. Was not that your phrase?"

"I have sinned," said the girl, "but don't talk of it. Henceforth I belong to the sentimentalists. But you must not spoil my plans. I must get to the top and wait devoutly on the tertium quid. You can wait here or go round the foot and meet us at the other side. You have made me feel sceptical already."

"I am at your service, my lady, and I hope you will get good news from the fairy-folk when…"

But at this juncture something held the speech and eyes of both. A figure came wildly over the brow of the hill, as if running for dear life, and took the slope in great bounds through brake and bramble and heather-tussock. Onward it came with frantic arms and ineffectual cries. Suddenly it caught sight of the two as they stood at the hill foot, the girl in white which showed dimly beneath her cloak, and the square figure of the man. It drew itself up in a spasm, stood one moment in uncomprehending terror, and then flung itself whimpering at their feet.

V

The full history of the events of these minutes has yet to be written. But such is the rough outline of the process of disaster.

It appears that the farmer of the Lowe Moss was driving his sheep in comfort with the aid of his collies, and had just crossed the meadowland and come to the edge of the Knowe. He was not more than half a mile from home, and he was wearied utterly. There still remained the maze of tree roots and heaps of stones known as the Broken Dykes, and here it was hard to drive beasts even in the clear moonlight. So as he looked to the far lights of his home his temper began to break, and he vehemently abused his dogs.

Just at the foot of the slope there is a nick in the dyke, and far on either side stretches the hazel tangle. If once sheep get there it is hard for the best of collies to recover them in short time. But the flock was heading right, narrow in front, marshalled by vigilant four-footed watchmen, with the leaders making straight for the narrow pass. Then suddenly something happened beyond human expectation. In front of the drove the figure of a man arose as if from the ground. It was enough for the wild hill sheep. To right and left they scattered, flanked in their race by the worn-out dogs, and in two minutes were far and wide among the bushes.

For a moment in the extremity of his disgust the farmer's power of thought and speech forsook him. Then he looked at the cause of all the trouble. He knew the figure for that of a wandering dealer with whom he had long fought bitter warfare. Doubtless the man had come there by night to spy out the nakedness of his flock and report accordingly. In any case he had been warned off the land before, and the farmer had many old grudges against him. The memory of all overtook him at the moment and turned his brain. He rubbed his eyes. No, there could be no mistaking that yellow topcoat and that scraggy figure. So with stick upraised he ran for the intruder.

When the Earl saw the sheep fleeing wide and an irate man rushing toward him, his first impulse was to run. What possible cause could lead a man to drive sheep at night among rough meadows? But the next instant all hope of escape was at an end, for the foe was upon him. He had just time to leap aside and escape a great blow from a stick, and then he found himself in a fierce grapple with a thick-set, murderous ruffian.

Meanwhile the shepherd of the Redswirehead and the tailor of Callowa had left the high road and tramped over the moss to the Knowe foot. The tailor's wine-begotten bravery was somewhat lessened by the still spaces of country and the silent eye of night. His companion had no thought in the matter save to get home, and if his way lay over the crest of the Fairy Knowe it mattered little to him. But when they left the high road it became necessary to separate, if the correct fashion of the thing were to be observed. The shepherd must slacken pace and make for the near side of the hill, while the tailor would hasten to the other, and the twain would meet at the top.

The shepherd had no objection to going slowly. He lit his pipe and marched with measured tread over the bracken-covered meadows. The tailor set out gaily for the farther side, but ere he had gone far his spirits sank. Fairy tales and old wives' fables had still a measure of credence with him, and this was the sort of errand on which he had never before embarked. He was flying straight in the face of all his most cherished traditions in company with a godless shepherd who believed in nothing but his own worthiness. He began to grow nervous and wish that he were safe in the Callowa Inn instead of scrambling on a desert hill. Yet the man had a vestige of pluck which kept him from turning back, and a fragment of the sceptical which gave him hope.

At the Broken Dykes he halted and listened. Some noise came floating over the tangle other than the fitful bleat of sheep or the twitter of birds. He listened again, and there it came, a crashing and swaying, and a confused sound as of a man muttering. Every several hair bristled on his unhappy head, till he reflected that it must be merely a bullock astray among the bushes, and with some perturbation hastened on his way. He fought through the clinging hazels, knee-deep in bracken, and stumbling ever and again over a rock of heather. The excitement of the climb for a moment drove out his terrors, and with purple face and shortened breath he gained the open. And there he was rooted still, for in the middle a desperate fight was being fought by two unearthly combatants.

He had the power left to recognise that both had the semblance of men and the dress of mortals. But never for a moment was he deceived. He knew of tales without end which told of unearthly visitants meeting at midnight on the lone hillside to settle their ghostly feuds. And even as he looked the mantle of one blew apart, and a glimpse of something strange and white appeared beneath. This was sufficient for the tailor. With a gasp he turned to the hill and climbed it like a deer, moaning to himself in his terror. Over the crest he went and down the other slope, flying wildly over little craigs, diving headlong every now and again into tussocks of bent, or struggling in a maze of birches. Then, or ever he knew, he was again among horrors. A woman with a fluttering white robe stood before him, and by her a man of strange appearance and uncanny height. He had no time to think, but his vague impression was of sheeted ghosts and awful terrors. His legs failed, his breath gave out at last, and he was floundering helplessly at Miss Phyllis' feet.

Meantime, as the young man and the girl gazed mutely at this new visitant, there entered from the left another intruder, clad in homespun, with a mighty crook in his hand and a short black pipe between his teeth. He raised his eyes slightly at the vision of the two, but heaven and earth did not contain what might disturb his composure. But at the sight of the prostrate tailor he stopped short, and stared. Slowly the thing dawned upon his brain. The sense of the ludicrous, which dwelled far down in his heart, was stirred to liveliness, and with legs apart he woke the echoes in boisterous mirth.

"God, but it's guid," and he wiped his eyes on his sleeve. "That man," and again the humour of the situation shook him, "that man thocht to frichten me wi' his ghaists and bogles, and look at him!"

The tailor raised his scared eyes to the newcomer. "Dinna blaspheme, Jock Rorison," he moaned with solemn unction. "I hae seen it, the awfu' thing – twae men fechtin' a ghaistly battle, and yin o' them wi' the licht shinin' through his breistbane."

"Hearken to him," said the shepherd, jocularly. "The wicked have digged a pit," he began with dignity, and then farcically ended with "and tumbled in 't themsel' ".

But Miss Phyllis thought fit to seek a clue to the mystery.

"Please tell me what is the meaning of all this," she asked her companion.

"Why, the man has seen Callowa, and fled."

"But he speaks of two and a 'ghaistly combat'."

"Then Callowa with his usual luck has met the spirit of the place and fallen out with him. I think we had better go and see."

But the tailor only shivered at the thought, till the long shepherd forcibly pulled him to his feet, and dragged his reluctant steps up the side of the hill.

The combat at the back of the knowe had gone on merrily enough till the advent of the tailor. Both were men of muscle, well matched in height and years, and they wrestled with vigour and skill. The farmer was weary at the start, but his weariness was less fatigue than drowsiness, and as he warmed to his work he felt his strength returning. The Earl knew nothing of the game; he had not wrestled in his youth with strong out-of-door labourers, and his only resources were a vigorous frame and uncommon agility. But as the minutes passed and both breathed hard, the younger man began to feel that he was losing ground. He could scarce stand out against the strain on his arms, and his ankles ached with the weight which pressed on them.

Now it fell out that just as the tailor arrived on the scene the farmer made a mighty effort and all but swung his opponent from his feet. In the wrench which followed, the buttons of the Earl's light overcoat gave way, and to the farmer's astonished gaze an expanse of white shirt-front was displayed. For a second he relaxed his hold, while the other freed himself and leaped back to recover breath.

Slowly it dawned upon the farmer's intelligence that this was no cattle dealer with whom he contended. Cattle dealers do not habitually wear evening clothes when they have any work of guile on hand. And then gradually the flushed features before him awoke recognition. The next moment he could have sunk beneath the ground with confusion, for in this nightly marauder who had turned his sheep he saw no other than the figure of his master, the laird of all the countryside.

For a little the power of speech was denied him, and he stared blankly and shamefacedly while the Earl recovered his scattered wits. Then he murmured hoarsely –

"I hope your lordship will forgi'e me. I never thocht it was yoursel', for I wad dae onything rather than lift up my hand against ye. I thocht it was an ill-daein' dealer frae east the country, whae has cheated me often, and I was vexed at his turnin' the sheep, seein' that I've had a lang day's wander." Then he stopped, for he was a man of few words and he could go no further in apology.

Then the Earl, who had entered into the fight in a haphazard spirit, without troubling to enquire its cause, put the fitting end to the strained relations. He was convulsed with laughter, deep and overpowering. Little by little the farmer's grieved face relaxed, and he joined in the mirth, till these two made the silent place echo with unwonted sounds.

To them thus engaged entered a company of four, Miss Phyllis, the Sentimentalist, the shepherd, and the tailor. Six astonished human beings stood exchanging scrutinies under the soft moon. With the tailor the mood was still terror, with the shepherd careless amazement, and with the other two unquenchable mirth. For the one recognised the irate, and now apologetic, farmer of the Lowe Moss and the straggling sheep which told a tale to the observant; while both saw in the other of the dishevelled and ruddy combatants the once respectable form of a friend.

Then spoke the farmer : –

"What's ta'en a' the folk? This knowe's like a kirk skailin'. And, dod, there's Jock Rorison. Is this your best road to the Redswirehead, Jock?"

But the shepherd and his friend were speechless for they had recognised the laird, and the whole matter was beyond their understanding.

"Now," said Miss Phyllis, "here's a merry meeting. I have seen more wonders tonight than I can quite comprehend. First, there comes Mr Grey from nowhere in particular with a plaid on his shoulders; then a man with a scared face tumbles at our feet; then another comes to look for him; and now here you are, and you seem to have been fighting. These hills of yours are worse than any fairyland, and, do you know, they are rather exhausting."

Meantime the Earl was solemnly mopping his brow and smiling on the assembly. "By George," he muttered, and then his breath failed him and he could only chuckle. He looked at the tailor, and the sight of that care-ridden face again choked him with laughter.

"I think we have all come across too many spirits tonight," he said, "and they have been of rather substantial flesh and bone. At least so I found it. Have you learned much about the future, Miss Phyllis?"

The girl looked shyly at her side. "Mr Grey has been trying to teach me," said she.

The Earl laughed with great good nature. "Midsummer madness," he said. "The moon has touched us all." And he glanced respectfully upward, where the White Huntress urged her course over the steeps of heaven.

John Buchan

The Courts of the Morning

South America is the setting for this adventure from the author of *The Thirty-nine Steps*. When Archie and Janet Roylance decide to travel to the Gran Seco to see its copper mines they find themselves caught up in dreadful danger; rebels have seized the city. Janet is taken hostage in the middle of the night and it is up to the dashing Don Luis de Marzaniga to aid her rescue.

Greenmantle

Sequel to *The Thirty-nine Steps*, this classic adventure is set in war-torn Europe. Richard Hannay, South African mining engineer and hero, is sent on a top-secret mission across German-occupied Europe. The result could alter the outcome of World War I. Other well-known characters make a reappearance here: Sandy, Blenkiron and Peter Pienaar.

JOHN BUCHAN

THE LONG TRAVERSE

This enchanting adventure tells the story of Donald, a boy spending his summer holidays in the Canadian countryside. John Buchan knew that some Indians were said to have the power of projecting happenings of long ago onto a piece of calm water.

In this tale he chooses Negog, the Native American Indian, as Donald's companion and guide. Negog conjures up a strange mist from a magic fire and brings to life visions from the past. Through these boyish adventures peopled with Vikings, gold prospectors, Indians and Eskimos, Donald learns more about history than school has taught him.

THE SCHOLAR GIPSIES

John Buchan wrote these sixteen essays as a young man. They have as a common theme his love of the classics, literature and the outdoors. And as Buchan says in his introduction 'they were written in close connection with that most beautiful country, the upper valley of Tweed, where the grace of old times seems to have long lingered.'

The tales are peopled by tramps, gentlemen of leisure, fishermen and wanderers, whose free spirit Buchan admired. The changing landscape with spring's arrival is beautifully captured in *April in the Hills*. In *Afternoon* a twelve-year-old boy plays at being a Jacobite and dreams about his future and the adventures he plans.

JOHN BUCHAN

SICK HEART RIVER

Lawyer and MP Sir Edward Leithen is given a year to live. Fearing he will die unfulfilled, he devotes his last months to seeking out and restoring to health Galliard, a young Canadian banker. Galliard is in remotest Canada searching for the River of the Sick Heart. Braving an Arctic winter, Leithen finds the banker. Leithen's health returns, but only one of the men will return to civilization.

THE THIRTY-NINE STEPS

John Buchan's most famous and dramatic novel presents spy-catcher Richard Hannay. Hannay is in London when he suddenly finds himself caught up in a dangerous situation and the main suspect for a murder committed in his own flat. He is forced to go on the run to his native Scotland.

Printed in Great Britain
by Amazon